I0650375

Harry Bennett Edwards

A Tantalus Cup

Vol. III

Harry Bennett Edwards

A Tantalus Cup
Vol. III

ISBN/EAN: 9783337066611

Printed in Europe, USA, Canada, Australia, Japan

Cover: Foto ©Andreas Hilbeck / pixelio.de

More available books at **www.hansebooks.com**

A TANTALUS CUP.

A Novel.

BY

MRS. HARRY BENNETT-EDWARDS.

" Art is long, and Time is fleeting,
    And our hearts, though strong and brave,
Still like muffled drums are beating
    Funeral marches to the grave."
                    LONGFELLOW.

IN THREE VOLUMES.

VOL. III.

London:

SAMUEL TINSLEY & CO.,
10, SOUTHAMPTON STREET, STRAND.
1879.

A TANTALUS CUP.

CHAPTER I.

ELLIS stayed at the Langham Hotel all the next day, waiting and hoping for Zaré's coming. As she had laid aside the passion for gambling, and followed him to London, she would not surely be driven away because she had seen him bending over Enid, and holding her hand in his. He argued :

If her love was so strong as to have brought her to his side when she had vowed to devote herself to play for the winning back of her *palazzo* and all its treasures ; if in the face of this enticement she had torn herself away from it all, and come back to him, she would surely conquer the less irresistible passion of jealousy. Less irresistible ! Ellis did not know that of all the passions with which the spirits of evil have endowed a woman, there is none so irresistible as jealousy. It seizes upon her body and soul, it turns her brain, distorts her mind, poisons her whole system. She is mad. A jealous woman knows no more what she is doing than the poor maniac in the asylum ; or if she knows, she does not care, which is the same thing. She will walk straightway into the midst of the fire, if she fancies that she can cause her enemy an extra torture by standing at her side and being consumed with her. There is no imagining too un-reasonable, no absurdity too gross, to encourage the growth of that fetid fungus —jealousy. It comes to maturity in a night; not one shoot, but twenty; they grow and spread, and poison the beautiful plant on which they appear, till it becomes loathsome to behold.

Yes, she is mad, the woman whom jealousy has cursed with its presence. She is more dangerous than the drunkard, for spirits bring feebleness at last, but jealousy super-human strength; she is more to be feared than the maniac, for you cannot put her in chains, and shut her out from all contact with other men. She is free to kill her thousands; there is no law against such murder as she commits; she may slay husband, children, parents, herself. She

does slay them; she drops the poison into
the cup of their life's happiness, till they die.
She starves her children for lack of the love,
the care, the protection for which they cry
to her, while her whole thoughts, her whole
energies, are directed to nursing and feeding
her own jealous passion. She is a murderer.
She curses her husband's life till he raises
his hand against himself or her; not the hand
of flesh and blood perhaps, but the hand
which brings death in life, the hand of moral
desperation, the suicidal hand of recklessness.
It may fall upon himself, or her, or both; its
ruinous strength is unlimited. She does not
care; he has wronged her!—some one has
wronged her! it matters not who—she will
be avenged!

But worse than all, the poison of jealousy
makes blind its victim. She cannot see

whether there be cause or no cause, whether truth or fancy gave it birth; she cannot reason or accept demonstration; no light can penetrate the jealous brain but the hideous green and yellow light of its own reflected ugliness.

It is the bane of all society.

It is the great blot which stains and blurs so many women's beauty. It is the curse of our sex. Let us fight against it.

But Zaré never came. Ellis spent the day with Enid; they lived in the past again, in perfect unity of thought and oneness of spirit. Only the love element was wanting; for Ellis was glad to feel himself a friend, and a friend only. The lover had been a difficult part to play, save on a few rare occasions. But he discovered how truly she had loved him, he saw how she had moulded herself to the form he chose for her, how she had raised her mind to his standard, how she had worked and thought, and carefully trained herself in his ways. This did not pain him, for what he could not see was her constancy. That she *had* loved him, he had not a doubt; that she loved him still he never for a moment believed; he even thought she liked him less than of old, because of her cold distance of manner towards him, "Or perhaps," he argued, "he was so changed that she could not recognise her old playfellow."

He strove all the harder to please her; he wished her to think well of him now; he respected her opinion; before, he had never cared how she regarded him—she was a child then, and incapable of judging; she was a woman now, and, as he saw at once, a thoughtful, self-reliant woman, and mentally strong, although she did not wear blue stockings or spectacles. He scarcely knew her as the Enid of old. She was beautiful too, with, as Zaré had perceived, a calm Madonna-like beauty, eminently womanly, eminently pure; she was like Correggio's Magdalen, or, as Ellis chose to think her, like the Marguerite of Ary Scheffer.

He was true to his old faith in his artist-god, to the belief of his boyhood in its absolute purity. He had seen almost all of Scheffer's pictures now; he had compared them with those of other modern painters in England, France, and Germany, and still he held the palm leaf over them, still he bowed down before them and worshipped. His ideal of perfect beauty was still perfect simplicity, perfect spirituality; he would,

were it possible to him, forbid to art the
expression of the grosser human passions,
and render only the sublime immortal.
Such power was not his to wield; but he
looked forward to the attainment of it in
some future when his day-star of fame
should have reached its zenith, and unob-
scured should shine before all men high up
in the heavens. At present it was only just
peeping above the horizon.

He could not waste time staying on in the
hotel; he must find a studio and work. The
Academy would open in three months; his
' Mignon' must receive the whole of his time
and attention between now and then; it must
be worked up, and finished off carefully, and
in perfect tranquillity.

He did not intend to let Zaré's
absence disturb him; he believed she

would come back when her passion had
worn itself out.

He found a studio and a sleeping-room
which suited him, and he went away once
more to work and to struggle alone. But he
left his address at the hotel, so that if Zaré
sought him there he could be found.

Before Enid left, he showed her his
picture of 'Mignon'; she was especially
interested in it, for she had seen the
original conception as it lay in the old
washhouse at Littlefield. She had always
thought it a wonderful work—so, indeed, had
he, in those old days of his young aspirations.
To-day he laughed at his own boyish vanity
and at her ignorant admiration of all he
did.

'It will be so different now, Enid,' he had
said to her before showing it; 'the picture as

it stands is certainly better than my first
humble attempt at the execution of a difficult subject. But you will probably think
it inferior in every way to that poor daub,
which you, in your innocence, imagined a
work of art. Your better education now
will require a higher class of merit; probably
I shall not reach to your standard of worth,
and certainly you will *not* find in me the
perfection you attribute to an exaggerated
and unreal remembrance of my powers.
Prepare for disappointment.'

'I do not think I have over-estimated your
talent, Ellis,' she answered, true to her old
faith; and although he did not need her
encouragement now, it was sweet to feel the
presence of a loyal friend, the sympathy of a
true woman.

Sweeter still to listen to her praises when

she stood before the picture worshipping like a little sad-eyed saint at a shrine. She knew what she was talking about when she admired the bold freedom of the drawing, when she spoke of the soul of the picture; she understood the spirit of the conception, and felt its poetry. He experienced a more perfect joy at her sympathy with his work, than at all the admiration which had been lavished upon it by the leading artists of Italy.

As yet it was unknown in England; but the night was far spent, the day drew on apace, and Ellis Lyndon longed to see its close. After that he should know whether he were to live or die, for he was sure that in this, his first work, lay written his destiny. Alma Deroi had said so, and others echoed the prophecy.

Afterwards Ellis went with Enid to the station, and bade her God-speed upon her long lonely journey. She did not cry or utter loud regrets—the agony was too great; it was that silent expressionless misery which presses the life-blood out of a young heart, which robs young limbs of their strength and elasticity, which makes a woman old before her time, and brings grey lines in her soft brown hair.

But Enid could bear it—only the physically weak sink under suffering. Ellis went back to his painting, alone in the new studio.

There were a hundred people in London on whom he could have called who would have received him open-handed and open-hearted; but he wished to be quiet. He had seen enough of society in this one year of his married life; it had tired him mind and body;

he needed rest. He intended to read and study, a luxury he had not known since he left La Viola. He was even glad of Zaré's absence, since he firmly believed in her return to him in so long or so short a time. What she might do in his absence did not trouble him; he had never possessed the slightest influence over her outer life; her friends were not his friends, or his hers; he had never succeeded in so much as checking an extravagance or correcting a folly.

Her life would be the same, near or away from him. He laughed at her threat of moral self-destruction; she might lose her money—she probably would lose it before her passion for play should be satiated; but let herself down from her own standard—never!

Ellis almost hoped the crash would come soon; she could not gamble if she had

nothing to gamble upon; not to any great
extent, he supposed. But, in truth, he did
not yet know all the ways and means of a
dishonest passion.

So he worked industriously, painting
smaller pictures for sale, and spending his
leisure time on the 'Mignon.' As it grew
into perfection, he was more and more
content; he *felt* that it was worthy, that if
this did not find favour, nothing he could
ever do would bring him fame. The best
years of his life had been devoted to it, his
whole intellect had been concentrated upon it.
It *must* be admitted into the Academy—he
felt that it would. Once there, it must be
noticed, if for no other reason, for its very
unlikeness to anything else which had ever
appeared upon the walls; its strange neutral
colouring, and its blank objectless back-

ground. It was a large picture, too, and worthy of report; its appearance in public must make or mar him for ever. There would be no 'damning him with faint praise,' no shuffling between merit and demerit. It would be altogether cursed — unanimously, unreservedly—or it would be *the* work of the season, on everybody's lips, in everybody's thoughts, and Ellis Lyndon's name passing from end to end of the country. Ellis Lyndon, himself society's last new ingenious plaything, with which it would amuse itself for a while till something new were introduced for its diversion. Then perchance he would be tossed aside by the multitude, but surely picked up and treasured by the few who knew his real worth, by men who had not taken him at other people's valuation, but at their own—brothers in art, who would love him for his own sake, whether he were the fashion or 'only a great painter.'

And the time of his trial was drawing very near. Ellis was not excited about it; his temperament was placid enough now, when the sun shone upon him and illuminated all around him with its life-giving brightness. He was full of hope and confidence, believing in himself and in mankind. And so a month passed away, a quiet delightful month, in which he painted and read, and lived in a world of glorious thoughts. All day he wandered amongst the pictures of our public galleries, learning to know them, one and all, not with the mere superficial knowledge of the eye, but to understand their nature, that it might become one with his own.

Every evening he went to the theatre or

the opera. Zaré had taught him to love music, till now the harmony of sound and the harmony of colour seemed almost identical sensations to his mind, and inseparable one from the other.

A few friends of his later days had indeed found him out, but they were not society friends, and exacted nothing from him; they gave him the pleasure of their company occasionally, and asked for his in return. They were men who lived as he lived, and thought as he thought; whose presence was never an intrusion, whose society never wearied him.

Ellis was peacefully happy for that month; the whole dream of his boyhood and youth seemed to be realised. His life was one of purely intellectual enjoyment and exquisite refinement. He was absolutely content.

CHAPTER II.

But at the end of the month a letter came to him which put an end to his enjoyment of the luxury of quiet and independence. It was from Enid, and ran as follows :

' Dear Ellis,

' After my saying so positively that I would not write to you, it will surprise you to receive a letter from me, and its contents will cause you some astonishment.

' I am in Baden-Baden ; my employer the

Princess Nicoline of La Viola! Now perhaps you can guess the subject of my letter? Your wife is here, in this house, ill and helpless. For reasons of their own they will not write to you; they have some object in wishing to keep her under their power and apart from you. I cannot even guess what it may be. I had been in the house a week before I knew who was the invalid they talked so much about. Then one day they asked me to go and sit with her, saying that the familiar sound of an English tongue might cheer her, and they were going out for the evening. I went, and found your wife, but so changed I did not recognise her at first. Whether she knew me I cannot say; she did not appear to do so then, she does not now, and yet she looks at me so strangely sometimes that I cannot help fancying she

31—2

recognises me and will not confess to her knowledge.

'From the first moment she took a strange fancy to me, and insisted that I should be allowed to come and sit with her every day. Afterwards she would not go to sleep unless I was in the room with her; and so at last she has passed almost entirely into my care. On second thoughts, I feel sure she does *not* know me, Ellis; her mind is in too unsound a state. She cannot talk rationally, but only raves about some *palazzo* which she has lost, and which she means to recover. So far as I can gather, she has parted with a great deal of money at the gambling-table, and the loss has injured her brain. The doctor says it is only a temporary affection, caused by long continued excitement. I do not know, I can only tell you that she is confined to her room, and so physically weak that she cannot even stand. She seems to realise nothing that goes on around her, yet in some things shows a strange persistent obstinacy—and one of these is that no person but myself shall come near her.

'They try to be kind to her; but, Ellis, she should be under your care. I scarcely like to tell you that she has already tried once to put an end to her own life; luckily I was able to stand in her way—never mind how it all happened. Since that fearful night, she clings to me even more closely than before. She is like a child in my hands; I can rule her with a word; none of the others have the slightest control over her.

'You must come here and fetch her, remove her from amongst these people, who, though not actually injuring her, evidently encourage her to go on losing money, and will, as soon as she can leave the house, lead her back to the tables. This I know from their conversation. They fancy I do not understand Italian, nor do I well, but it is impossible, knowing something of the language, not to comprehend their actions and to see what is going on in the house. Your wife is evidently very ill, Ellis, and you must come to her at once. Be sure you do not mention my name, and you will greatly oblige me by treating me as a stranger if you see me here.

'For myself, I am very comfortable; they give me every luxury, and I am interested in my poor neglected little pupil. Her parents seem to ignore her existence; she is absolutely under my care. I have the command of her carriage and of her servants; she is a strange unnatural child, but I like her and would keep my place if possible.

'An acquaintance with you or your wife, if known to the prince or princess, might be objected to by them; at any rate, I would see more of them before I risk mixing my name with that of their friends. Mrs. Lyndon might object also, when she recovers consciousness. At present I am only the governess. Your wife knows nothing, and if you take her back to England with you she will never know.

'I am called Miss Smith here. I could not bear to hear my father's name on strange lips; don't forget that, should you have occasion to address me. Please do not write, Ellis, it might be dangerous; remember that I know nothing of these people. But come and take your wife away from them if

you wish for her welfare ; she is too weak to
resist you now. I heard them say that she
had left you on purpose ; I heard them praise
her determination not to go back to you.
I think they have some design upon her
property. But come and see for yourself ;
and, Ellis, I put you on your honour not to
betray our acquaintance. I have the strongest
reasons for this caution.

'Yours ever affectionately,

'ENID.'

'What a strange world !' Ellis thought,
'that in all the length and breadth of it, Enid
should have fallen upon the one spot from
which I would have held her back with all
the power of my influence over her—She
and the Princess of La Viola side by side !—
the girl I most respect, and the woman I most

hate ! What a horrible combination ! It must
not be ; in saving Zaré I must save Enid,
too. I will talk to her, tell her what these
people are, and get her to give up the
situation at once. Enid governess to the
child of that woman ! it is dreadful to con-
template !'

But his wife—She was ill, helpless, amongst
strangers. All his old love, forgotten of late,
seemed to revive at the thought that at last
she might require his help, his protection ;
that at last he should assume a husband's
proper place respecting her. That he should
no longer have to stand like a favoured
courtier near her throne, dependent on her,
obedient to her whims and fancies, accepting
everything from her, and giving nothing
in return. This thought had galled him
often, but he had said :

'I will give her the honour of a great name, that which she most cares for in this world; my success shall be hers, my fame hers; she shall value me as she values her pictures and her china—as something for the possession of which other men shall look up to her. This is the only return I can make, since my love is no longer enough to satisfy her.'

But now that she was ill; poor, probably, and dependent on him, he felt himself a better man, and a truer. He would go to her at once and take upon himself the burden of her feebleness, and of her support, if need be. He almost hoped that her money *was* gone; she could not go on playing if she were penniless. It was the hideousness of this vice which had well-nigh turned his love into disgust. He might yet care for her, as he had cared, as he still wished to care, if only the passion for play could be conquered. This illness might be the means of saving her; who can tell?

Ellis put together a few every-day necessaries; and started at once upon his journey, wishing to lose no time. He must be back in London within the week. There was much to be done yet in preparing his picture for the Academy, and only a few weeks in which to do it. They would be busy weeks, with a sick wife on his hands; but he had taken a rest, he was refreshed body and mind, the struggle would be a pleasure to him, the success doubly gratifying.

There was a great delight, too, in feeling that now at least some of the duties of manhood would devolve upon him, some of the burdens that marriage brings; some of its responsibilities. Ellis was not afraid to share in the common lot of mankind; he had only chafed and fretted under the slavery of poverty, in the chains of thwarted ambition; he had only kicked against the prison walls of his checked desires, only rebelled against his inability to move even one step forwards.

It would be easy enough now, out in the air and the sunshine, to travel along even with a burden on his shoulders, or a mill-stone round his neck; neither one nor the other could make him fall now; there were so few more steps before his journey's end. Up there on the hill-top—there lay his resting-place; close to him; 'He must reach it, happen what may,' he argued. So he journeyed forth to seek and to save the woman he had once so madly loved. All that was past now

—a fever which had gradually worn itself out; but he might be happy with her still.

Zaré was an intellectual woman, her mind, was equal and sympathetic with his, they had the same tastes and the same ambition. It were surely not possible that they could live apart for ever, or that together they could be unhappy, if she would only lay aside that one vice which was as a curse upon her?

Ellis Lyndon's present state of mind was one of confiding hopefulness; he would almost, like Zaré, have staked his dearest treasure on the goodwill of Fate towards himself.

A few English artists and judges of art had seen his picture now; they were unanimous in its praise : they encouraged him to hope for an unprecedented success, from the first moment he should stand forth amongst

them.   They might be flatterers, one and all.
Ellis did not put any faith in their prophecies;
but in his own sense of satisfaction, in his
own feeling that his work was worthy of the
pains he had expended upon it, worthy of
Alma Deroi's teaching, he *did* find the sweet
unction, which he laid to his own soul.   He
believed in himself now, and all the world
smiled upon him ; when he had doubted himself, the earth and the sky and the waters
had frowned pitilessly around his path.

'Dr. Osborn was right,' he said; 'as we
are internally, as our minds are balanced and
shapen, so are our external surroundings ;
they do but reflect our own lights and
shadows.   It were a poor philosophy which
cannot teach us that self-respect is the strong
primary ray which is reflected all around
and about us.   It is not conceit, it is not

vanity, that belief in the power of the mind or of the brain which nature has given to us. It is only when self-respect degenerates that it becomes base and despicable—when we would no longer *be* great in our own sight, but would only be *thought* great by others. When we know our own insignificance, but would not have other men know it; when we would appear what we are not—then, in truth, does self-respect degenerate into vanity. When we would have the world admire us for what we feel ourselves unworthy, laud us for what we know ourselves lacking—then only is self-respect a mere miserable conceit. Without self-respect we cannot rise—by pride we fall. They are in no wise akin one to the other.

Ellis Lyndon was neither vain nor conceited, but he esteemed himself so long as he could respect himself because of something he had done worthy of himself. But when he could not respect himself he was nothing, he despised himself far more than other men ever despised him. He made no false estimate of his own virtues, he did not wish any one else to overrate them. There were a few men whose good opinion he desired to possess, because he knew they would never give it dishonestly; but for the rest he cared not one jot. If the few believed in him, if he believed in himself, let the ignorant many condemn him how they would, it affected him not. He had no desire to come forward on the stage and to receive the applause of the gallery and the pit—no, nor of the private boxes either, except of one here and there which he could have pointed out to you.

Such was Ellis Lyndon in his early manhood, when the world prospered him, and all things seemed working for his good—even this, the apparent misfortune of his wife's illness and the loss of her money : if not all of it, at least a great part; enough probably to make his the hand which should lead them both in future, his the support on which they must both lean.

Men will understand his feeling. He had married Zaré in the thoughtless passion of a young love, which is truly pictured blind. He had not considered that her riches and his poverty must place him second to her in everything after the first month or two—he had not thought about it at all; he had only rushed into her arms with the mad joy of a satisfied longing, and lain there dreaming for a time.

Afterwards he awoke and found himself in her house, at her table, with her servants waiting on him. He was one of her belongings, to be cherished by her, and cared for, and cast aside if she grew tired of him. He tried not to feel the weight of the jewels he was forced to wear, since it was himself who had put them on, but they were unnatural, and they jangled unpleasantly as he walked about in them, till sometimes he fancied that everyone else must hear the noise and notice how out of place they were—nay, laugh at him for having accepted them.

It was not so in truth : men did not blame him when they looked into Zaré's eyes and heard the tone of her voice ; any one of them would have worn the chains Ellis wore, and deemed himself blessed—for a time—even as Ellis had done.

But all such delusions are momentary. Man was not created to sit at a woman's footstool and receive gifts from her hands; he would rather grind corn for her in the sweat of his brow, whilst she stands by and pays him with the golden thanks of her tender wifely love. There is honour in this, and manhood and pride. In the other, humility, and servitude, and degradation.

A man cannot stoop without dishonour; but a woman bows her head and bends her knees, and the sanctity of holiness glows glory-like around her.

After another day and another night had passed over, Ellis Lyndon found himself once more in the streets of Baden-Baden; once more his steps were turned towards the Princess Nicoline's house. It was as if nothing had changed since he last stood

on that spot—not even Zaré, his beautiful
self-willed wife, whom he had so often
loved and hated, blessed and cursed, in the
same moment of time. He felt nothing but
a tender pity for her now.

CHAPTER III.

THEY were in London again, Ellis and his wife, under the same roof which had covered them in the days of their early love, amongst the same Lares and Penates which they had worshipped together in the temple of the bright-eyed Venus. It was all different now. Through the halls, wherein the sounds of voices, music and revelry had been wont to echo day and night, there was silence; where the thousand lights had glowed and blazed till the morning sunshine put them to shame, it was cold and dark. The huge rooms were empty, upstairs and down. There were only three servants in the kitchens, and three persons in the sitting-rooms—Ellis, his wife, and the hired nurse who took care of her.

Zaré was very ill. But the physician in London echoed the opinion of his colleague in Baden-Baden, that hers was a temporary affection of the brain, the result of some intense and protracted mental excitement, and of great physical weakness. Her state was a most curious one. She knew Ellis, was conscious of what went on around her, and yet she would sit all day long doing nothing, with her hands clasped over her knees, and her large hollow eyes staring into vacancy. If Ellis addressed a question to her, she would stare up into his face for some seconds, and then, shaking her head, make one of two replies : either, 'It is no use to try and persuade me to the contrary; I will win back my *palazzo*, or die in the attempt. He cheated me; it was not my luck which failed—he cheated me !'—or she sometimes would say : 'If you think that you can blind me, mislead me, deceive me by soft looks and fond words, you are wrong; Zaré Landrelle never forgave an injury.'

And these, with variations of expression and wording, were the only answers he could ever get from her to questions far removed from the subjects.

Nevertheless, she liked him to sit in the room, and always inquired where he was if he were absent longer than usual. And yet, when present, she never spoke to him, or moved from her place, or expressed a wish that he should do anything for her. Three or four times a day she would say aloud, talking to herself:

'I am getting better, I shall be able to go back soon; he can't run away, he has promised to give me six months to win it back in; only half of that time is gone. I shall be well in a week or two now.'

Then she would get up, try to walk, stagger back helpless, and sit for the rest of the day like some grim figure carved in stone.

She was not beautiful now—far from it; her face was pale and haggard, there were silver lines in her hair, and her great dark eyes, with their wide-open stony stare, seemed to be all you saw of her face. You shuddered to look upon it, remembering what it had been. Ellis, when in Baden-Baden, had seen Enid alone for half an hour. He had tried to persuade her to leave the Princess Nicoline's service, showing her the kind of woman she was : a gambler, a drunkard ; a false wife, a heartless mother. But Enid only said :

'She will not contaminate me, Ellis ; I am too old to change now.'

She was still thinking of her love, and how that had altered her once ; but nothing which could happen now would have any effect upon her character, she knew. She told him, too, that the princess being such as she was, her unfortunate child needed a friend the more—some honest person to save her if possible from contamination, to sow good seed in the little empty mind, which should bear fruit in later days.

'Indeed, Ellis,' she said sweetly, 'I could not have found an occupation which would

suit me better. I like the responsibility.
The child has no other guiding power than
myself; her parents see nothing of her, and
that their responsibility may be the less,
they never interfere with me in any way.
I am absolute mistress of the little Princess
Loyella's domain and of herself. I am a
person of great importance, I assure you !'
Enid had concluded, laughing.

But Ellis saw that her eyes were
full of tears, and her sweet mouth
trembling sadly. He took her hand and
kissed it; he called her the truest, noblest
woman in the world; he told her that
so long as he lived she need never want a
friend, that as a brother she must come to
him if she found herself in any difficulty or
trouble.

Then he went away, grieved still at her

coldness towards him, at her utter want of sympathy in his affection. It was strange that he could not read the love which made her start and tremble at his touch ; strange that he could believe her cold, when her heart was burning with a cruel destroying flame ; but still it was so. Enid, little simple country Enid, had turned out a grand actress, a magnificent deceiver. She had said to herself :

' Since he never loved me, it were self-abasement and dishonour to let him see the endurance of my love for him. Better a thousand times that he should think it was a mere passing fancy, like his own. So I shall not blush to stand face to face with his wife.'

And she had played her part right well. She had not forgotten it, as too many women

do, just at the trying moment; she had not
said, 'I will deceive him,' and then taken
care that he should *not* be deceived; that
only her tongue should repeat the false
sentiments, while her actions showed him
the true, even though they were sentiments
which might be a dishonour unto him and
unto her.   No, Enid was not one of these.
What she set herself to do was perfectly
done.

So Ellis Lyndon left her alone in her new
country amongst her new people.   And he,
the man she loved so truly, went back, content, to England with his wife, whom Enid
knew now, too late, he could *not* love—
not, at least, for long.   Enid grieved for him,
and trembled for his future.   She had paid
dearly enough, hoping to purchase his happiness; and now she thought that after all

the bargain might be a bad one, and herself
the fool who had been duped into making it.
What if she had helped to ruin him by
throwing him into Zaré's power? What if
by her agency he should perish? The possibility was only another bitter pain for her
to bear in silence. And since she had seen
Zaré lying ill in that house, it had grown
into a probability—nay, to almost a certainty.
Enid saw that there could be no happiness
with such a wife. But she was powerless to
save him now.

In the meantime Zaré was in London.
She recovered slowly, so far as her mere
physical health was concerned, but as her
mental excitement subsided, as her brain
grew calmer, the apathy which had come
upon her of late increased to a dangerous
extent. She no longer raved, even about

her losses; she never spoke or moved, and yet her strength had almost come back to her in the last fortnight.

'She must be roused,' the doctors said; 'if once we can get her out of this state of insensibility, she will be quite well. If now something were to happen to work her into anger, or to put her in some great danger, anything to excite her nervous energy, you would find her strong enough. This apathy is a reaction following upon the state of excitement under which she has been labouring; both are unnatural conditions, and this one takes a more aggravated form than the other. What can we do to rouse her? You must think of something, my dear sir.'

But Ellis could do nothing; everything he tried failed, and she remained a lifeless, soulless, inanimate creature, impervious to all outward influences, and equally void of all inward consciousness, so it seemed.

Ellis despaired ; but whilst he was distracting his brain for some new means of bringing her back to life, there stood in his path once more the starry-robed goddess, spindle in hand, and she wove the threads of their destinies her own way, even towards the end she had mapped out for them.

It was the first of May, and the London season again. Carriages thronged the parks, people crowded the shops and the streets, dinners were given, and balls and soirées. But Zaré's house was empty still, and silent. Ellis had been working hard, money-winning, for he did not know how much or how little of his wife's property remained to her. None, according to the accounts of the Prince and Princess of La Viola. This he did not

believe. It was true Zaré had no money
in the bank, for he inquired, but there was
other property, he felt certain.

He had interfered so little in his wife's
money matters, that he knew not even the
sources from which her income sprang.
Anyhow, there was the house in which they
were living, and all its costly furniture; this
was hers, and her jewels, and her pictures.
But for the present he preferred to live on
his own earnings. There were dealers
enough now who gladly bought any small
pictures of his on speculation, having heard
of the probable—nay, certain success of his
first contribution to the Royal Academy,
which was already talked about in the world
of art.

He had taken to portrait-painting, too, as
a means of present income, but he did not

intend to pursue it ; it was, according to his idea, derogatory to art ; one of its lowest grades, utterly wanting in the sublime spiritual element of conception, in the poetry of imagination. ' In your picture you strive after perfect beauty,' he said. ' in your portrait you must paint what you see. A figure such as nature never made, a head grotesque, with impossible hair, and drapery at which the artistic eye closes, smarting under the effect of its harshness.

Ellis knew it were possible to idealise the woman of to-day, and make her a Phryne or a Magdalen, a Venus or a Gabrielle—but then it is not a portrait ; and where are the women who would be content to have themselves so transformed for art's sake ? Nevertheless for the moment Ellis stooped to paint a woman as he saw her, not accounting it a part of his art, but only a piece of mechanical labour, a means of earning money, a business.

The Prince and Princess of La Viola came to London with the rest, and their house in Hyde Park was the resort of all the fashion-able world—the world of frivolity and soulless vanity, the world of outward show and in-ward emptiness, the flattering, fawning, lying world, which licks the feet of a title and worships money as a god ; the world which never asks ' What manner of man is this ?' but only ' Who is he ?' which never says ' What does he do ?' but only ' What kind of dinners does he give ?' He is a prince, an earl, a duke ; that is enough !—He gives dinners once a week, with real turtle, and port a century old !—Who need inquire further ?

Such was the world which crowded round the Princess of La Viola, and bowed down to her and worshipped her. Its people believed themselves amongst the highest of England's noble blood and proudest birth. They would have stared at you, and laughed, and pitied your ignorance, had you told them that away in the quiet country homes, in the nurseries of their children, by the fire-side of their husbands, there were greater far than they. That the purest blood and the proudest lineage of our land is not to be found in the crowded salons of London, fawning at the feet of princes, or thronging round them in the parks.

Amongst the rest, the Princess Nicoline was told that she ought to see the wonderful picture painted by quite an unknown artist, a Mr. Lyndon, about whom 'people who

33—2

LIBRARY
UNIVERSITY OF ILLINOIS

knew' foretold great things.   It would be
sent up for judgment to the Academy in a
fortnight; in case of its being hung and
noticed, it were as well to have known
something of it before, to have predicted its
success, to be able to say, 'Ah, yes! I said
so when I saw it in the studio.'

'It was very difficult to get a private view
of it,' they told the princess; 'the young
artist had only shown it to a few special
friends; but if the princess knew him or his
wife, poor creature! she should make the
most of the acquaintance, and profit by it.

'Oh, yes! she really must see the picture.
She could tell them all about it!'

Accordingly she went to call on 'The
sweet dear Zaré, whom she loved so well—
so well!—poor beautiful angel!'

Ellis was not at home; and Zaré, when

asked whether she would see the princess, nodded her head, as was her habit now, instead of speaking. Accordingly this friend was shown up to the boudoir, the only sitting-room used now in all that large house. How empty and desolate it seemed ! The princess shivered as she mounted the staircase, remembering what it had been last year. When she entered the room, Zaré did not move or lift her eyes off the ground. The princess sat down by her side, she laid her hand on Zaré's arm.

'Are you glad to see me, my own darling sister?' she said, speaking in Italian. 'I have been pining for you, but your husband would not let me come to you. He is keeping us apart, Zaré. Do you hear what I say, *cara mia?*—your husband is keeping us apart.'

That was the first poison drop; it made Zaré start and look up and say :

'Yes, I had forgotten; you are right, you shall see me soon, I will come to you.'

This was not what the princess wanted; *she* had no desire for the charge of an invalid in her house just now, when so much company called for her attention. She changed her tactics.

'No, no, stay here till you are quite well —quite strong—till we can go out together and enjoy ourselves as we used. If you begin again yet, you will lose your head again, and then—adieu to the *palazzo*. Pietro does not wish to keep it—he cannot bear the thought; he will give you every chance to win it back; he is waiting for you, but you must take care of yourself, keep quiet for a time, and grow strong—you understand ?'

'Yes, yes, you are right,' sinking again into the apathetic state of a moment ago.

The princess could get no answer from her on any ordinary subject; life seemed to have lost all interest for the Zaré of to-day. But there was yet another poison drop to follow the first. It must be administered. Zaré must not be allowed to forget, or all the princess's schemes might fall to ruin.

'And your husband,' she whispered, bending over Zaré; 'is he good to you? Has he given up the girl he loved, and taken the sweet Zaré back to his heart?'

For a moment this shaft seemed not to have pierced through the dulness of her brain.

The princess was despairing, but presently

it struck the mark.   Zaré's eyes flared up
with the sudden blaze of a smouldering fire,
and she said :

' How can I tell? what do I care? would
you have me ask him ?'

' No, no ; I was foolish, the question was
absurd.   Of course, of course! you have been
ill, they have kept you up here far away
from him ; you cannot know who comes to
his painting-room, or where he goes.   I
might have thought — pardon me, my
darling.'

There was no want of life in her now—

Zaré sprang up, and fixed both her claw-
like hands on the princess's shoulders.   It
was as if some wild cat had flown upon her,
and was spitting in her face ; she became
frightened at the glare of Zaré's huge eyes,
and at the glisten of her teeth.

'You know something,' she hissed; 'tell it to me, or I will kill you.'

'No—no, I do not know anything,' gasped the princess in her terror.

Zaré released her, but stood ready for another spring.

'Then what did you mean to imply?'

'Nothing. Calm yourself, my sweet sister, or you will fall dead; you are not strong. I say the truth; I *know* nothing; I have not seen, I have only heard that some girl, young and sweet-looking, visits him often in his painting-room. But you can find out the truth; you are not a prisoner, you can walk, and see, and hear. When any visitors come, watch them; if what people say is not true, then you are content; you will forgive his past, and be happy with him always—always, as I would see my sweet Zaré, and rejoice greatly.'

The princess had heard nothing about Ellis, for there was nothing to hear. But it was a part of her scheme to keep alive the flame of jealousy which burned so fiercely in Zaré's nature ; the hell-fire which could transform a woman into a fiend, the blaze which would destroy her, and leave the Princess of La Viola master of the field. She cared not whether Zaré should see or not see any woman by her husband's side, it was enough to keep awake suspicion, and the fire would feed itself. She had done what she intended to do, and she rose to go.

'She would call again to see the picture,' she said, 'if the beloved Zaré was too tired to come downstairs and show it to her.'

But Zaré did not feel tired now; a new strength was in her limbs, a new energy in her brain. The stimulus for which the doctors wished had been given, and its effect was such as they predicted. Zaré went downstairs for the first time, and showed the princess Ellis's picture.

And whilst they stood looking at it, a new expression came over Zaré's face. It was triumphant, and yet agonised; the features were contorted, and the brow was contracted, but the lips were smiling, and the eyes glowed with a horrible pleasure—glowed as the eyes of a cat who watches the poor mouse she has half killed making vain attempts at escape — A new thought had entered her brain, born of the words which the princess had just spoken—But nothing more was said. The princess lavished the profusest praises upon the work before her, and ended by saying:

'But my sweet Zaré must not allow herself to fancy that because a woman would love that wonderful work of her husband's hand, they would love or be prone to love himself. No, no; many women will come to see it, even as I have done; many will worship it for its own sake; Zaré must not fancy they are here from any but the purest motives, as lovers of art, not of men. Zaré must not be suspicious of *all* the women who visit this studio; she must blame only where blame is due; she must be sure of her enemy. Will she promise?'

And so the poison drops fell one by one till the princess had exhausted her store, and noted, well pleased, the effect they took.

'I never make mistakes,' Zaré had answered, in her old proud way, and then this friend left her—The one woman she had always loved as a sister, the one she had trusted ; in whom alone she had confided, believing her true if all the rest were false.

So little do we know of each other !

CHAPTER IV.

ELLIS sat alone in his studio. It was the day after the Princess Nicoline's visit to Zaré ; he noticed the change in her, and wondered whether it were for better or for worse. He watched her restless eyes, wandering into every corner of the room, he saw how nervously she twisted her fingers in and out of each other, he noted her flushed cheek and red lips—She looked almost like herself again.

Instead of sitting still from morning till night in one chair, she wandered perpetually in and out of the room and up and down stairs—her restlessness frightened him. What could the princess have said to her to work this change? Ellis could only fear that it was a return of the old gambler's excitement, aroused in her by the sight of her companion. He wished he had been at home when the princess called; he would have refused her admittance into his house at any cost.

Well, the doctors had said Zaré must be roused—it was done effectively now, but Ellis doubted how far it would benefit her really; doubted whether she would ever be quite well again, there was something so unnatural about her altogether. And yet he could not call her mad; she knew what she did, and what others did around her; she fancied nothing different from what it was, except where her jealousy misled her. But

this was such an old, old story now, that
Ellis never heeded it.

So one day he was dreaming fair dreams,
sitting before his picture doing nothing, but
thinking a world of sun-illumined thoughts.
What a strange, changeful life his had been
since he left Littlefield! never the same for
six months together. He had trodden in
the black slimy mire of poverty, and it
stained his feet and soiled his whole being;
he had put on silken hose and fine raiment,
and walked in the palaces of kings, and it
had purified him. With burning brain and
throbbing pulse he had lived the fulness of
life, drinking deep in the intoxication of its
sweetness, till earth seemed to him heaven,
and heaven a hell, because it was not earth.
He had worshipped in the temples of the
Muses, at the high altars of the Gods; he

had held the banner of Excelsior in his hand, and climbed almost to the mountain top. The ascent had been easy, for he only trod in the footsteps of greater men who had preceded him, making straight the way before him. And now he was waiting awhile to rest before commencing the last, the steepest piece of all; to think before stretching forth hand and foot towards that highest point from which would be revealed to him all the kingdoms of the world and the glory of them.

Repose was easy to him, for Zaré would not allow him to do anything for her; she treated him with a cold contempt and disdain, as one who had done her an irreparable injury. He was not much grieved—there was in his heart too little love for the woman he had married; passion had filled its place

once, and now passion seemed dead within
him. He was wondering whether it would
ever live again for Zaré or for any other
woman, or whether his art would henceforth
be the only creature he should worship blindly
and on bended knee, the only object of his
life's devotion. He felt that it must be so,
and yet—he was human, he was young; he
could not take to his heart, to fondle and
caress it, an unresponsive creation of his own.
His nature was eminently sympathetic, but
from childhood sympathy had been denied
him. The lack of it had gone well nigh to
ruin him once; it might do so again.

Even Enid cared nothing for him now, he
thought; he might die or fall, no one would
regret him. His pictures could not shed
tears. Often he had cursed the loneliness of
his lot, often he would have changed places

with the blue-necktied, gold-pinned, red-
handed youths whom he saw day after
day in the parks side by side and hand in
hand with their rosy-faced, sweetly-smiling
peasant loves—women who, at least, looked
up to them, trusted them, believed in them.
Such devotion Ellis had always coveted; it
was the one thing which had been denied
him. He had fancied Enid's love of this
kind, but to-day he found it like all the rest—
a thing of the moment, an amusement.
After all, what did it matter? When he
possessed it he had not cared about it; why
should he regret its loss? Nevertheless, he
did regret it. He was grieving over it
to-day as he sat alone in the studio; it was
the one blast of chilling wind which made
him shiver in the glow of this summer sunshine. Presently the servant came into the

34—2

room and brought him a written message
which, he said, some lady waiting at the door
had sent up to him.   She wanted an answer.

Ellis read it :

'If you are quite disengaged and alone, I
would speak to you on a matter of business.

'I am waiting below.

'ENID.'

He desired her to be shown up, and smiled
almost one of his old satirical smiles at the
notion of his little friend with a 'business'
on hand.   But he was right glad to see her.

She came in very demurely and shook
hands with him, and sat down by his side on
the round ottoman.

'Enid, my darling child, what have you
done to yourself?' was his greeting.

He spoke as in the old days, meaning nothing; but she started and grew paler still. In truth, he was frightened, the change in her was so marked. All her girlhood seemed gone; she was a middle-aged woman, thin and pale, with drooping head and tiny white hands, through which the blue blood-vessels showed in delicate threads. She seemed to him like a wood-lily which had been transplanted and was withering in the new soil. She was beautiful with the beauty of his dying Mignon, there in front of them; a spiritual, poetical loveliness which was not a substance, but only an essence of her being; a sentiment unexpressed, but palpable to the senses.

She could not answer him for a moment, and to gain time she pretended to be tired after a long walk. He offered her refreshment, but she would accept nothing. In another minute she had recovered her self-possession, and was able to school her voice into obedience to the part she must always play before him, even to the end of their days.

'I came on a matter of business, Ellis; something concerning your wife and the Princess of La Viola—You ought to know it,' she said, with perfect composure.

'Ought I? Well, it will keep I suppose. After not seeing you for so long, do you think I am going to talk about other people? Tell me something of yourself, child.'

'But I came for that and no other purpose; I must tell you!'—rather more hurriedly.

'So you shall, presently; I'll take you home, and on the way we'll talk *business*,' he smiled one of his sweetest smiles, and she felt as if heaven were open before her. 'For the present you will tell me about yourself; and first—What makes you look so ill?'

'Oh, never mind me; I am not ill—it's only the air of cities makes me pale. We are going to La Viola in July, I shall be better then. Is that your picture?—the Mignon, I mean?' she said, rushing into another subject.

She could not endure his notice of her altered looks; she was so cruelly conscious that her hopeless love, her anxiety for him, her yearning to see him, was the source of her ill-health. She could not sleep, because his presence haunted her; she could not eat, because sleep had forsaken her. She was ill, she knew it, but that he should notice it was

an agony she could not endure.   There was
a cloth hanging over the picture; she went
and lifted it up as an excuse to turn her face
away for a moment.

'Yes, I want your opinion on it now it is
finished,' he said, removing the cover, and
turning the picture to the light.

She stood before it entranced.   She forgot
herself, his presence, everything in the
rapture of her delight.   It was not because
the picture was grand that she worshipped it,
but because it was his work, a sign of his
greatness; it told her she had not been mistaken in him, even when she was an ignorant
country child.

Enid was no art-worshipper for art's own
sake; she had studied it for his sake, to be
equal with him, to understand him, but it
was only as it affected him that she regarded

it. The Mignon represented his mind, his thoughts; it was the faith he taught, the religion of purity and simplicity and truth. It was to Enid a thing sacred as the Bible to the Christian, a gift direct from God, a mighty, imperishable inheritance which would make Ellis Lyndon immortal.

She was an idolater still, you see, but she worshipped in perfect faith

As she stood before the picture, with her folded hands hanging down in front of her, white upon her black dress ; as her eyes were raised prayer-like to the dying Mignon's face; as her lips were parted, and her quick breath came and went in short, excited gasps, *she was a living reflection of the figure on the canvas before her.* There was all the sunset glow of perfect peace which had come to her in that moment of self-forgetfulness when

she lived only in his success, in his greatness.
The same expression as awoke into a new life
the broken heart of the dying Mignon ; glori-
fying the last moments of her earthly existence.

And, after all, Enid had suffered much as
she did. A sublime love, true as hopeless,
and hopeless as true ; something to be crushed
out, and buried, and trodden under foot ; the
worm which, gnawing at the roots of the
plant, destroys it at last ; the blight which
withers all its green leaves, and nips the buds
from their stem, till there is nothing left but
gaunt, lifeless branches, through which the
wind whistles drearily.

Ellis noticed the resemblance.

' I wonder,' he said, coming up to her side,
and resting his hand brother-like on her
shoulder, ' I wonder whether I have uncon-

sciously painted your face in that picture? I did not intend to do so ; I had believed it originated in poor Lizzie Grey. So it did, but I have altered it so often, taken so much away, added so much, according to the fancy of the moment, that it has lost its identity with her. Look yourself, Enid,' he held out his hand and pointed towards it, ' those are your eyes, the mouth is yours, and the pure, sweet, womanly soul is yours.'

She smiled, and the tears welled up into her eyes. He did not see them; he was intent upon the picture—and she on him.

Neither of them turned away from it, or they would have seen standing at the door, which was wide open, Zaré, with blazing eyes and glowing lips, with clenched hands and glistening teeth, watching them and listening to the words he spoke. Zaré, magnificent in her anger as a tiger in its lair, waiting its time to spring upon an unconscious enemy.

But when he was silent, Zaré stole away noiselessly as she had come, and went slowly up the broad staircase ; the carpet was so soft that the sound of her footstep had not reached the ears of Ellis and Enid, in either her coming or going.

For some minutes neither of them spoke ; at last he said, dropping the curtain over the picture once more :

' Well, do you see yourself, or is it only my fancy ?'

' Your fancy,' she answered, forcing a smile.

She would not see it. The thought, if harboured, were as a spray of ether falling over her, bewildering her brain, and making her fancy glorious things which never were and never would be. If he had painted her, he must have had her in his thoughts, she must have possessed them to the exclusion of other things. No—no! let her rather dash away the sweet cool poisonous drops, and feel the pain of the reality. He had not painted her; it was but a fancied resemblance, one of those momentary likenesses which we see for a second, and never again. 'Twas but the association of two ideas; there was no truth in it. But there was danger. Enid felt it, and made her escape.

'But, Ellis,' she said suddenly, 'I did not come here to amuse myself or you—I came solely for your wife's sake. She has fallen into the hands of enemies; you must get her away from them.'

'You might as well ask me to remove the

earth out of reach of the sun's attraction, one were quite as possible as the other. But I want a walk, I am tired of sitting still ; we will discuss this *business* '—with a sneer—' in the open air. It will be quite like old times again, we two side by side. I have not to go upstairs, my hat is in the hall. Come along ! I don't think you had better see Zaré ; she would recognise you now, and——' he hesitated, then laughing, ' and, although you didn't suspect it at the time, she was rather jealous of you once.'

' What do you mean, Ellis ?' she flushed angrily. ' Jealous ! I beg you will not say that word again ;' then, seeing him look hurt, ' I mean, you men make use of such absurd terms, we don't quite understand them. For the moment I was taking Dr. Johnson's meaning and application of the term jealousy—

I did not make allowance for modern license ; only please be more careful what you say.'

She had corrected him ; he had no right to tell her of his wife's follies—he felt it so ; he had merited the reproof.

'Forgive me, Enid,' he said, holding the door open, and they both passed out into the street, where the business which had brought her to his studio was immediately entered upon by Enid.

She had only come to him with one object, to attain one end ; the rescue of his wife from her enemies. Enid did not know how small was his influence over that wife ; judging by herself, she fancied he must be able to control any woman, and to lead her whither he would.

She was even yet a child, worshipping on bended knee, with folded hands and upturned eyes, the great, unapproachable spirit into whose hands she had once given the keeping of her life.

She could not take it away again now.

CHAPTER V.

ZARÉ listened at the top of the stairs till she heard the front door shut behind them. Then she went into her bed-room, and turned the key, locking herself in.

She did not seem particularly excited, but some firm purpose impelled her; she hesitated about nothing, neither did she hurry or appear confused. First she opened her wardrobe, and taking out the richest dress which hung there, she put it on.

A deep purple velvet, trimmed with lace old, and rich, and costly; such a costume as few women would have dared appear in by daylight, but Zaré was always proud to defy slander, and to wear or do what she liked. When dressed, she hung massive dead gold chains about her neck, and at her throat; in her ears and on her wrists she wore wonderful ornaments of strange workmanship, gold also, but so curiously fashioned that they would attract notice anywhere as rare things, the like of which was never seen before in England—wonderful remains of some bygone time. Leonardo Landrelle had given them to her as a wedding present; he accounted them of priceless value.

So decked, Zaré stood before the silver-framed mirror and looked at her haggard face; she smiled in derisive pity, on her own ugliness.

'We can soon touch up and revarnish the

old picture,' she said aloud, 'it will appear as good as new; there are fools enough in the world to be taken in by it yet.'

She opened a box, and with infinite pains and marvellous skill laid the colour on her cheeks and lips, and made the yellow, withered skin look young and clean once more.

It was quickly done, and a new creature stood there: a beautiful woman with a queenly carriage and a haughty curve of the neck, the Zaré of old—One degree less startling than before, perhaps, one shade less perfect, for false colours had to supply the place of real ones, which once they had served only to subdue or to heighten as required. It was necessary to wear a veil to-day, to hide the unreality of her face.

At last she was ready to go out. Not a single detail of her toilette had been neglected, She was perfectly dressed. Then she found a hand-bag, and into it she crowded all the jewels from her dressing-cases, all the laces from her boxes, laid some necessary clothes on the top of them, and locked it up.

Afterwards, she took one last look round, stood for a moment thinking, and went down-stairs, carrying the bag with her.

She entered her boudoir, and seating her-self at the writing table, penned a letter, which she put into an envelope, addressed it to her husband, and stood it on the mantel-shelf, making it as conspicuous as possible, so that he could not avoid seeing it on entering the room.

This finished, she pulled out a side drawer and took from it a penknife—a gold-handled, jewelled thing, which had been made for ornament, not use ; but it would serve her purpose. She examined the large blade carefully, passing her thumb over the edge to feel its keenness. Yes, it would do her bidding.

' Its first use will be an important one,' she thought, wondering why she had been so foolish as to buy such a toy only because it was pretty to look upon.

Then she locked up the desk, and carried the knife in one hand and the bag in the other outside into the passage. The door of her husband's studio was opposite to her, wide open, as she had left it.

She went into the room, and shut the door after her softly, as if afraid of disturbing some one, or of scaring some poor harmless ghost she had expressly come to look upon.

And, in truth, the place was haunted with

the presence of her husband and Enid Osborn, as Zaré had last seen them. Their voices, in sepulchral tones, seemed to chant the words she had heard him speak to her as he stood on the spot she now occupied, with his hand resting on Enid's shoulder, pointing out to her the expression which lay in the eyes of the Mignon and in her own.

' The love-light !' Zaré hissed through her clenched teeth ; ' even I could discover that.'

Then she lifted the cover and stood for a moment looking at the picture.

' If *she* had not loved you, I would,' Zaré said, addressing the Mignon in self-justification, ' for you are the grandest conception I have seen produced since the days when Correggio's hand guided the brush to a like purity of truth. Yes, you would bring him fame, if I

would let you, if I would bow my head and
be trampled upon, and allow *her* to glory in
his success. He told me that her hand had
held him up once ; let it do so again, if it can.
We will see who has the most power over
his destiny, she or I ; whose hand can make
him rise or fall ; who can destroy and who can
save ; the honour of one were as great as the
other. 'Tis but a battle of the angels and
the devils over again ; the devils always conquer in the end ; their victory is as glorious
to them as the angels to themselves. No
quarter is asked or given on either side.
Victory proclaims itself in the result—If he
fall, the day is mine ; if he rise, she shall have
the honour of his salvation. Let her set the
power of her love against the strength of
my hatred, and see which shall conquer. I
would have been true, for I loved him, fool

that I was ! 1 would have led him onwards
and upwards, and placed him safely amongst
such men as had given him his reward. I
would have triumphed in his triumph, gloried
in his glory, bowed down to him and worshipped. But not she ; never shall she say,
" See what I did for him by my constancy
and truth ;" never shall he say to her, " This is
your doing, Enid ; you predicted my greatness, you believed in me when I did not
believe in myself, you bade me hope and fight
and conquer. See, it is done "—No, never!
I, Zaré, will stand between them ; I will say
to them, " Fools ! with one stroke of my
hand I can send his soul to hell and his body
to destruction—See me make it." '

She laughed aloud as the last thought
formed itself into half-spoken words, which
were as a curse called down upon him.

Then she went close to the picture, and raising the hand in which she held the open penknife, she forced it into the canvas and slit the picture from top to bottom. After-wards, she cut it deliberately from corner to corner, till it hung before her—a mass of rags dangling from a golden frame! Her work was done; she replaced the curtain over it, setting it straight and smoothing it carefully.

She left the room, shutting the door behind her.

In the passage she took up her bag, went downstairs and out into the street. She hailed the first cab which passed her, and was driven away somewhere. No one knew, no one cared; she had become a nonentity of late.

Out in the world, or at home in her own house, Zaré was nobody now; she, who had for several seasons been the leader of fashion, the brightest diamond in a coronet of gems of the purest water in the world. Hers had not been a sham lustre, her surroundings no spurious imitations of the stones they would represent; she had chosen them well, from a perfect knowledge of their worth, and she valued them accordingly. But she had passed from amongst them—and they so easily replaced her with another diamond, no less brilliant, no less costly. She was forgotten, quite forgotten, as though she had never been.

It is the fate of all society's darlings. Society treats them as it does a popular novel. For six months they are in everybody's house, on everybody's tongue, in everybody's thoughts; lauded to the clouds, picked to pieces, abused, envied, imitated—

for a season. Then something fresh comes
out, something startling, and the traitors
flock to the new standard. They forget the
poor old book, and all the poor old characters
in it, which had caused them so much
pleasure last year. Already it is getting
soiled and worn, it disfigures their drawing-
room tables, it is put aside on a shelf, no one
opens it again.

No one cares for silvered hair and lack-
lustre eyes, for faded cheeks and withered
lips. But they have had their day, so let
them not complain.

When Ellis returned to the house, he went
at once to look for Zaré; he must tell her
what Enid had just told him, he must make
one more effort to part his wife from the
Princess of La Viola. Surely, if Zaré could

be persuaded to believe all that he could tell her to-day on Enid's authority, she would mistrust her seeming friends for ever afterwards—she would discover their object in fawning upon her and flattering her. She would accept this warning.

Ellis was surprised at finding her out ; she had not left the house once since he brought her into it. He supposed she was gone to return the Princess's visit.

On the mantelshelf in the blue satin-covered boudoir he found her letter. This is what she had written :

' I have left you again, and for ever this time; it is no good for you to follow—I shall not return. I saw you with Enid Osborn to-day in the studio. But *I have taken my revenge.* Ten years hence, ask yourself who has had the most power over your destiny, she or I. You said you believed in *her* influence over your life—perhaps you will believe in *mine* for the future. Zaré was never slighted or set at naught with impunity, never from her earliest childhood. I have no more to say. You will not see me again. It is her move now; let her put her poor king out of the way of my " checkmate " if she can !

'ZARÉ.'

'She's mad !' Ellis said, tearing up the letter, and tossing the pieces upon the table with a contemptuous jerk.

This absurdity of hers angered him ; he must treat it as a mania or a joke. It were a sorry jest for her, since it drove her to such folly. She must be mad ; he would believe her so, and pity her. She could not harm him now; his only fear was that she might injure Enid, she and the princess together, if they joined forces against her.

" For there is no evil which the tongue of a jealous woman will not inflict upon her enemy,' he said. But still he did not fancy that Zaré would stoop to mean and petty injuries. She might murder Enid, if she came in her way, but he did not think her the kind of woman to undermine another's character, to back-bite her and to slander her.

'She must know that Enid is blameless,' he argued, and so he set aside her threats as the meaningless ravings of a brain diseased.

He had nothing particular to do that evening, so he went to the theatre. It was a favourite play of his, ' The Lady of Lyons.' Ellis had always felt the deepest sympathy

with Claude Melnotte : his passionate love
for an object so far removed from him, the
ambition born of that love, the despairing
agony of a great mind scorned because it
sprang from a peasant stem—all these things
in the character of Claude Melnotte seemed
to harmonise with Ellis's own nature.

Circumstances had made his life different
in degree from that of the poet hero of the
story, but the same tone pervaded both.
They could both be good men and true, if
not thwarted by prejudice, or goaded by
falsehood and insincerity; or they might
both become fiends, incarnate devils, once
fairly encompassed by the throes of narrow-
minded prejudice, and tortured by injustice
and suspicion.

But indeed Claude Melnotte's sublime love
was a truth which lay not in Ellis's life. He

had once believed himself capable of a grand poetic affection, such as would outlive passion, but his life had not proved its possibility. From the first he had known that his fancy for his little peasant-model was but a boyish romance. From the first he had felt sure that his infatuation for Zaré was a passion only. From the first he had seen that with Enid it was gratified vanity which led him to care for her, and afterwards a sincere brotherly affection.

None of these had been the mainspring of Claude Melnotte's love for his Pauline—a love which, though having its birth in a passion, could yet lay aside its grosser nature, and rise pure in its sublime grandeur. A love which could say to the victim it had brought to its feet : ' Arise, I will not accept thy sacrifice till I prove myself worthy of it ;' and so he would go forth to fight for the crown, that he might place it on her head.

No such love had never come to Ellis Lyndon, yet he still believed himself capable of experiencing it, and his whole soul went out in sympathy with Bulwer's self-made hero.

He went home that night feeling a better man for the impression it had left upon his heart, a truer for the softness and the tenderness of thought now succeeding to a certain cold dulness of sentiment which had crept over him after reading Zaré's letter.

When he came home, he sat up writing late into the night, and the tone of his essay was gentler and more merciful than was his wont. He dealt more softly with human weakness, he believed more firmly in human strength, and he went to bed thinking

kindly of poor Zaré and her disordered brain ;
wishing that he had been gentler with her,
and had tried more persistently to make her
love him, even when he saw her passion dying
ut.   .

And so he slept, dreaming only of the
triumph which was to be his in one short
week more, when they should have received
his picture into the judgment-chamber of
England's honour, when they should have
accepted it and have crowned him with his
laurels ; when the summit of his ambition
should be reached, and he could rest awhile
from his labour.

They were fair dreams, and glorious to
look upon. No shadow of the morrow
darkened their brightness. It were a pity
he should ever awake. If there were mercy
in nature, she would have laid him in his

grave ere he should open his eyes upon that ' To-morrow, and to-morrow, and to-morrow,' which ' Creeps in this petty pace from day to day, to the last syllable of recorded time.'

Well for him if he had never proved that ' All our yesterdays have lighted fools the way to dusty death.'

CHAPTER VI.

ELLIS LYNDON was feeling strangely happy that morning, as he breakfasted alone in the boudoir. It was the only room they had used since he brought Zaré back to London sick in mind and body, and he took his meals there as usual, now he found himself alone again. He was, however, making plans for leaving her house so soon as the fate of his picture should be decided.

It was a glorious spring day, and London seemed to smile upon him, to bid him come forth into her streets and her parks, and make himself one of her gay crowd. It was a day to be idle in—to sit still and admire what other men had done for your gratification; to look up at England's palaces and down at her vast subterranean city of life and bustle and industry; to ponder on the kingly state which the one held within its walls, and on the strength of the people out of whose brains the other had sprung, by whose hands it was worked, by whose courage sustained. A time to look proudly around at the wealth of the nation, to glory in her prosperity, and to feel the heart swell with the patriot's love of his strong sea-girt isle—A moment when every soul must experience the desire to add one more stone to the imperishable pile of England's treasures, one more name to the list of England's immortal heroes.

Ellis Lyndon intended to give up this one day to rest and amusement. But before sailing out to idle the hours away on the bright glancing waters, with his little ship in full sail, catching the soft breezes, and rocking him to sleep, secure in the safety of his craft, he must have one fond look at the source of all this dreamland of bliss, at the work which had occupied him mind and body for the last five years, *and was now complete* —a thing of beauty that all men might behold. His child, created by himself, brought to maturity by his hand, endowed by his mind with all holy attributes, beautiful, pure, true. There was no vain-glorious conceit in this love; had it been the work of another man, and, such as it was, Ellis Lyndon would have gloried in it, and without envy have acknowledged its transcendent merit.

He opened the door of the studio. It was the room he loved best in all the house, his sanctum, the high altar of his gods, and he the priest who worshipped there. He pulled the purple velvet arm-chair in front of the picture, turned it unto the light which he had chosen for it—Then he lifted the curtain —*A mass of rags dangled before him from a gorgeous gilded frame !*—Nothing more.—No beautiful form, no soft colouring, no eyes looking life-like into his own—nothing but a few strips of canvas daubed over with paint.

Ellis did not move—the hand which held up the curtain seemed petrified, as if it were the Medusa's head, serpent-crowned and hideous, which had been displayed to his sight. He stood like a man carved in stone : motionless, sightless, dumb, with fixed wide-open eyes and parted lips. Time was nothing to him, nor place, nor existence. He had no consciousness of anything beyond the horrible fascination of the mutilated creature before him. How long he stood thus no one ever knew. At last there was one great crash which echoed through the empty house, and Ellis Lyndon lay senseless upon the ground at the feet of his murdered child.

So they found him later, when they came to announce a visitor—so Fred Galway met his cousin once more after a separation of two years; called on him, only to take him in his arms, lifeless still, and carry him to his bed—Fred Galway, resplendent in trousers of a larger and livelier check than ever, in spotless patent leathers and lavender kids, with gold-headed cane, and a button-hole sprig of geranium and maiden-hair. He asked where Mrs. Lyndon was; the servants told him she had gone out to pay a visit yesterday and had not returned. Fred took upon himself to send for the doctor, Ellis was so long insensible. The doctor suggested that his patient must have fainted, and in falling have struck his head; there were undoubted symptoms of congestion of the brain—he must be carefully watched. Fred Galway said that he was a relation and he would not leave the sick man until Mrs. Lyndon's return. Accordingly, he took off his hat and gloves, drew the arm-chair to his cousin's bed-side, rang for the servant, informed the man of his intention to nurse his master in the absence of Mrs. Lyndon, gave him a sovereign, and repeated to him the doctor's orders.

Phillips was much astonished, but this cousin of his master's was evidently ' A *real gentleman,* some person of consequence, no doubt. It would be as well to submit quietly to his presence in the house ; of course, Mrs. Lyndon would soon return.' Such was the argument of Phillips, with the sovereign in his hand ; such was *not,* however, the opinion of the cook, who received nothing. Fred Galway's opinion he kept to himself, divining pretty clearly that ' something was up,' as he expressed it, and he did not at all expect to see Mrs. Lyndon come home, neither did he intend to leave his cousin to the mercy of servants. These were ' Jolly comfortable quarters !' and he ensconced himself in them uninvited. The servants made a feeble

objection; he quieted them with a clever
story about his having called to see his cousin
on a matter of business. 'A question of
£20,000 or more! it was necessary that he
should be by their master's side, to get a
signature to a document so soon as he should
be able to sit up—One day's delay would
be fatal!'—This was a pure invention, but
the servants believed him, because he was
wise enough to back his statement with a
'tip' all round. The doctor, too, said it was
necessary some friend should be with his
patient, so the prudent domestics submitted
to Fred Galway's mastership with a fairly
good will. They were beginning to see that
something *had* gone wrong, since their
mistress did not return. Altogether, it was
rather exciting.

Fred Galway was flourishing just now—

flourishing with ' " *The Seraphic* " *Music and
Dancing Rooms,* Sole Lessee and Proprietor,
Frederick Orlando Galway, Esq.,' as stated
in the prospectus.   But it was in truth Galway and Company, or more strictly Company
minus Galway, for Galway was only an out-
sider.   They paid him to lend his name, to
appear before the public as the proprietor, so
that in case of failure he would be the
responsible party.   The public could never
make Fred Galway pay, for the sufficient
reason that he had never a penny in the
world to pay with.   But he did not complain,
and he managed to enjoy his life.   How it
was all arranged does not matter to us, did
not matter to Ellis Lyndon, who probably
owed the saving of his life to Fred Galway's
watchful care, which day or night never
flagged—to the clever hands which did the

doctor's bidding, even as a woman might have done it, and with more than a woman's tact.

For many weeks Ellis Lyndon hovered between life and death. It was a long and painful struggle, because he had no wish to live. He wondered why they could not let him die quietly. ' What is the good of putting off for so many days or years longer an inevitable evil ?' he questioned, ' what can be the use of such a life as mine must be ? every hope, every desire, every ray of ambition gone, vanished into air, non-existent, as though they had never been.' He should only creep on from day to day, even with the dust ; he should exist, as the frogs and the toads exist on the margin of the black silent pool ; with never a sight of the blue sky, never a wish for the sunlight, content to grovel in the mud, and to snap greedily at the miserable flies which fall drowning before their noses. Truly, a life worth purchasing this! But he had no choice in the matter—his time was not come, his destiny still unfulfilled.

After a month of tedious illness he was able to move about again. He was a ruined man, shattered in body and in mind—soulless, heartless, objectless. Like a poor beast, he lived on from day to day only because he could not die. With the destruction of his picture, the whole fabric of his life had been cut in pieces; his heart-strings were snapped asunder with the threads of his canvas. And a wife's hand had wrought the devastation!—a hand he had kissed in passionate love! the hand from which he had looked for support across the field of his ambition. 'If an angel had come unto him,' he had not believed that Zaré could do this thing—Zaré, whose gods were pictures, whose religion was art, whose priests were artists. She had proved herself a dastard to her own faith. ' She must be mad !' he said again.

But mad or sane, she had ruined him for ever. There is no power on earth which will strike a man down to the ground so quickly, or so irrevocably, as great desires and noble aspirations suddenly torn from their dwelling-places, amidst the agony of the shedding of our heart's life blood and the stopping of our life's pulsations. If we die we are saved. If we live through it we become what our unleavened nature, our brute origin may make of us ; creatures ruled by desire, governed by impulse ; animals living on from year to year only to satisfy the lusts of the flesh. Such is a man after his fall. A few rise again, but it much depends upon the amount of the injury they have sustained ; a broken arm or leg is mendable, but a crushed spirit, torn up at the roots of its being, does not often throw forth fresh leaves.

From having been morose and satirical, Ellis grew cynical and misanthropical. From having believed in himself, trusted himself, and felt himself worthy of better things, he sank into an utter lack of self-respect or self-esteem, a state of absolute moral decadence.

When Fred Galway, who had heard the history of the destruction of Ellis's 'Mignon,' said, trying to cheer him :

'But, my obstinately dejected cousin, you have hands left, and a head too, if appearances don't belie you. Brushes, colours, and

bits of rag are not yet extinct species.
Begin a new picture, and by the time it's
half finished, you will thank your stars
number one never came before the public
number two will be so *vastly superior*.
Nothing like practice, you know, for making
perfect.'

'No—I shall give it up. That was the
one great inspiration of my life; I shall
never reach to the same height again.
Nevertheless, I could have gone beyond it
with that as a starting point—but not now.
When a man has lost his only child, the
one creature in whom all his hopes were
centred, the thing he had loved and clung
to for years, the future in which his life
was built up, he cannot console himself with
the idea that another child may be born to

him some day.   The loss of the one has
crushed him, he goes away into voluntary
exile to bear his grief alone.'

' Thereby cutting his own throat, and showing his extreme weakness of judgment, my
son.   If he stayed quietly at home now, a
few years would bring him a dozen more
of those innocent treasures, those animated
" Mignons ;" he could hang them all over his
room, and let the best of them go out into
society as his representatives, till at last the
fat and satisfied paterfamilias, sitting snugly
in his arm-chair, would rub his old capon-
lined belly, and wonder how he was ever content with one.   " And after all, on second
thoughts, a very poor one too," says he, compared with all those which are now around
him, and those which are winning for him
the praises of men out of doors—Ellis, my

boy, I'm sorry to use strong language, but— You're a fool.'

'I have come to the conclusion that Midas was happier than Socrates. The one had no more serious difficulty in life than the hiding of his ass's ears, the other had to fight against the decadence of a nation, his country's injustice, and in the end to die by the hand of ignorance and superstition. He would have done better to have given up struggling, thrown himself upon the mercy of his accusers, and lived for the rest of his days like a pet lap-dog, with no desire beyond the satisfaction of his own belly. He would only have forfeited the admiration and praise of a few fanatical followers after his bones lay rotting in the ground, and gained in exchange the substantial and palpable good of a quiet life, and an easy regretless death.'

'I say, old fellow, were you ever treated to a rotten egg for breakfast?' Galway asked seriously, screwing up his right eye at the corner. 'It stinks rather, don't it? That's a mercy, or one might put a mouthful of it down "unbeknown," as my friend Sairey Gamp says — The result would be unpleasant—Now, the pervading odour of your conversation happily warns one not to swallow it too readily. Like the egg, it's in a state of rapid decomposition.'

'And, like the egg, it were better pitched out into the gutter, so that the shell which contains it be smashed into a thousand fragments, and no man will ever turn to notice them.'

'Wrong, my dear fellow, wrong; somebody would get the benefit of it—and that wouldn't be fair you know. But seriously,

what are you going to do ? your available
cash is running short.   You must make the
missis *fork out.*'

' I would rather die than accept a gift from
the hands which ruined me.   I shall never
see her again.'

' Nobody wants you to ; but you have your
rights ; perhaps you forget that the money is
yours by law.'

' No—thank heaven it is not.   Her first
husband left it settled upon herself, absolutely under her own control and in her
own gift ; that much I do know about her.
I shall emigrate.'

Fred Galway burst out laughing.

' Emigrate ! well you *have* come to
the end of your resources.   Your brain
is not quite as fertile as I had once
fancied it.'

'Can't you see, man,' Ellis answered impatiently, 'that my only hope of not going to the devil altogether is to fly to the relief of physical exertion, to work day and night in the sweat of my brow, to tire my hand and to exhaust my strength with hard labour. I don't wish to sink so low as to become an object of pity to my fellow-men. If I stay here I shall.'

'By Jove! if it wasn't for the "Seraphic" I'd go with you—But you don't think of starting yet?'

'Not for a week or two. What use could I make of these puny shaking hands, or these muscle-less arms?—Heavens! how proud I was once of my biceps.'

Ellis smiled one of his bitterest smiles as he recalled the old days at Littlefield, and how conceited he was then of his muscular strength—later, how secure in the faith of his own mental power—And now there was nothing left of it all, nothing but feeble emaciated limbs and a brain distorted by hideous imaginings.

His hopes had been crushed on the eve of their fruition, his affections had been chilled and driven back upon himself again, even as in the loveless days of his childhood. A mother's hand had cast into the fire his first picture, so proudly accomplished after so many fruitless attempts—she had had no pity for his childish agony of disappointment; and now his wife had completed the ruin then begun.

As a child he swore that he would never draw again, and he kept his oath for a child's eternity—a year or two. Now again he cried out in the bitterness of his spirit, ' I was cursed from my birth ; my old nurse said truly that the devil stood godfather to me ; let him claim his own, I will struggle no more. If I starve, so much the better. Who will care? not even Enid now; she has other interests. Dr. Osborn is dead, thank heaven ! he will not see my fall— and for the rest I am accountable to no one.'

Thus he argued. But one hope — one desperate hope of rescue—clung to him still. He might have a relapse, his enfeebled brain might fail to bear the burden of its own misery : he might die. Or some sudden accident might fall upon him, and plunge him at once into eternity. Not that he believed in' such a state now. Annihilation —utter annihilation—of all the human race, with its intellect and its works ; annihilation of the whole universe, was his present faith.

'What makes us suppose we are immortal?' he argued in his bitterness of spirit; 'on what is our belief based? Does not everything on this earth resolve itself into its ultimate atoms? are not these atoms reabsorbed and reproduced under other forms —forms which can be measured and weighed and calculated, but all a part of the earth from which they sprang? What makes us presuppose a higher *individual* existence? Have I any knowledge of what went before? Do I know in what condition my soul existed previous to its present state—if, indeed, it did exist—and *to be* eternal, my soul must *have been* from all eternity. I have no knowledge of any former existence; it was not individual, it was not I, Ellis

Lyndon, it was not myself, it was nothing that is a part of my being, nothing that is identical with me as I know myself. Why should my future be otherwise? Why should it not be non-existent as my past? Why may I not be a part only of some great whole, working towards some end, one and the same with the trees and the plants; the earth, the planets, the suns—atoms of the universe?'

But let us stop here. We will not say how he argued, or what he brought himself to believe; how little of all that is elevating to the human soul, of all that raises man above the brutes; how poor his faith in any higher destiny than the mere fertilisation of the soil, how weak his trust in an Almighty ruling power. It were profanity to set down the thoughts of a tortured spirit, weary of its own existence. We know, you and I, and all of us, that there are moments in almost every life when goodness seems a meaningless term, when faith appears a ridiculous credulity, when truth seems so impossible of demonstration that it becomes non-existent for him who doubts, because he has not succeeded in finding it.

Let us judge Ellis Lyndon mercifully. His was a nature eminently sympathetic; he was absolutely dependent upon the sustaining power of some other nature which, comprehending his, would mingle itself with him and become a part of himself. It was necessary to him to feel that some one had faith in him, some one trusted him; for then he could make it a point of honour not to betray that trust, not to crush that faith. He only valued himself in so much as he was valuable to some other kindred spirit.

If no one thought him worthy, he could not think himself worthy ; he *was not* worthy. And yet, with this strange dependent nature, he had always been an alien from any perfect human sympathy. Enid had been one with him, but not he with her ; he had never felt her equal with himself, and perfect sympathy cannot exist without perfect equality ; the balance must be equal on both sides, that neither shall fall short of the other. Zaré he had only loved with a passionate intensity, and Dr. Osborn—was dead.

There was yet one other person who had come across Ellis Lyndon's path, and left a shadowy spiritual form behind him, an influence of softness and sweetness, of peace and beauty, a perception of the presence of a truth—the truth of a noble nature. Ellis had not seen much of Alma Deroi, but enough to feel that the purity of such a spirit could not fail to leave some ennobling influence in any life it had once handled with its gentle loving touch. Whilst he was his teacher, Ellis had been conscious of expanding in the reflected warmth of his perfect simplicity of nature, of being more generous, more tolerant, more merciful to the weaknesses of men less mentally strong than himself.

But Alma had left him when the influence was only beginning to make itself felt. It had passed off since, and Ellis now stood utterly isolated. I say stood; I am wrong, he could not stand—he fell—fell with a great moral crash at the moment when his physical strength gave way and he lay upon the ground on the grave of his murdered hopes, on the sod of his thwarted ambition, side by side with the remains of his desecrated picture.

A long illness had saved him from immediate self-destruction; he could not be desperate in his bed. For some time afterwards physical weakness kept him out of moral danger. He was strong again now—not, indeed, with the old buoyant strength of his youth, but the disease had left him. Yes; and a worse had succeeded it, one that only a miracle would cure: a desperate recklessness of life, an utter scepticism of everything, a misanthropical unwholesomeness of temperament—seeds which had been planted in him by the hands of his parents in the earliest days of his misconstrued childhood; seeds of which a few here and there had sprung into life whilst he was yet a boy, and flourished and ripened in his manhood. But their growth had been prevented in later life. A soil in which they could not exist had suddenly been poured over their heads—a soil as congenial to his true and better nature, as killing to his adulterated and unworthy one. For a month or two new and beautiful plants had sprung into being in the garden of Ellis Lyndon's life. These were spreading far and wide, and bearing good fruit, when the whole fertile plain was suddenly made a desert by one blast of a pitiless blighting wind. And underneath the desert sand lay the old, old seeds which thoughtless hands had planted there long ago.

Nothing kept them down now; they forced their way at once to the surface, and their shoots were even now appearing full of life and strength. Dangerous fungi, which there would be no destroying, let them once fairly usurp the ground.

Ellis knew this, but he did not care. 'No one else cared, why should he?' We do not value our lives for the good they bring to ourselves; we require some one else to share our satisfaction, some one else to praise us. Not, indeed, in long-winded phrases of adulation, but with the silent soul language of a loving eye turned upwards to our own, glowing with a heartful contentment, the silent grasp of a hand which in words 'more perfect than speech' says, 'Let us rejoice together, for your life is mine, your triumph mine, your thoughts mine.'

'These things alone make success worthy of a struggle,' Ellis said; 'they have been denied me one and all, and a curse laid upon

me in their stead, the curse of a lonely loveless life.'

And so he went forth and plunged head-
long into that burning glowing Lethe of
excitement which runs through every city
in every land, inviting the heart-sick and
the desperate to come and bathe themselves
in its waves; so shall they find oblivion, so
shall they forget the past, forget everything
in the intoxication which for a moment
the taste of its water lays over their
senses.

To-morrow those same drops will seem
bitter, to-morrow they will revolt the tongue
which touched them; but to-day they are
good! they are glorious! they send memory
—'the warder of the brain'—to sleep,
they—

'Raze out the written troubles of the brain,
And with some sweet oblivious antidote,
Cleanse the stuff'd bosom of that perilous stuff
Which weighs upon the heart.'

Yes ! *for a moment !—for a moment !*

CHAPTER VII.

When Zaré ran away from the deed which she had done in the madness of her jealousy, she disappeared from the sight of all who knew her. For six weeks she was not seen or heard of. Where she went, or what she did during that time no one will ever know ; but she recovered her health and her beauty, and one day she drove up with her old magnificent display to the door of the Princess Nicoline's house in London.

This was not what the princess had wished, but she was obliged to appear pleased at the coming of her 'dear sister,' as she called Zaré. It was of the greatest importance for the carrying out of a scheme which was already in working order, that Zaré should think well of her, believe in her, and hold her a true friend till the end.

The end! it has an unpleasant sound—but it did not mean bloodshed. The princess certainly had decided on an end towards which she was steadily working, but 'Her own hand would never be raised against the lovely Zaré—oh, no!'

'Only she was so excitable, so brave,' the princess said, 'there was no knowing how soon, in some access of passionate disappointment, she would make an end of her life. The poor reckless sister! She had never got over the loss of her lovely *palazzo*; it was cruel

of fate, oh ! so cruel, but it was Zaré's own
doing, she should not have challenged the
inexorable goddess.'

Thus the Princess of La Viola argued,
and she pursued her plans with her natural
wily cunning.

And so it came to pass, that when Zaré
arrived at the princess's house in London,
there was great apparent rejoicing at her
coming, and the best room was appointed
for her use ; whilst in secret the cleverest
maid was set as a spy upon her, and her
every movement recorded.

Zaré's health seemed as good as ever ; the
one great excitement had acted upon her as
the doctors said it would. It had given the
first motive power to renewed action, and so
broken the spell of her apathy. Yet she was
not the same ; there was a wildness in her

eye, and a restlessness in her movements, which had not been there in the Zaré of old—an utter recklessness of life, which was none of nature's doing ; for nature takes care of herself, holds out her hand to ward off evils, and treads in safe places.

Education alone teaches us that there is an end of suffering, that the sooner this end is reached, the sooner are we free from the burden of our life. And so some of us walk recklessly towards it, while others stretch forth their own hands to bring it nearer. But, alas ! neither nature nor education bids us beware of a greater punishment still for our crime, something harder to bear than the suffering we would escape. The one is a present and absolute evil, the other an un-proven possibility. We do not realise a here-after, we only accept it upon faith ; we who are strong, can act upon our belief—we ask no external proof, we are content with an internal conviction. Not so the weak—they require demonstration, we can give them none ; they say : ' Show us the fire, and we will not walk into it, we will not plunge into eternal destruction to escape an earthly torture which we know can only pursue us for a short span of time. Only make us *certain* of this retributive justice, and we will keep ourselves guiltless.'

We fail to prove it to them—and they laugh in our faces. We say, ' Behold *our* peace,' and they answer, ' Your lot has been cast in pleasant places,' or ' Nature made you unsusceptible ; your nervous organisation is not so finely strung as ours, or the action of your brain is more under your own control ; it is no virtue in you to support your

burden and carry it patiently to the end of
your journey. You were given a strong
back, and we a weak one, let us alone ; if
we tremble and cower under our burden, we
will lay it down and find relief.'

We hear them speak thus, we shudder at
their future, we pity their weakness, and we
cry out to God, 'Give us some power to
demonstrate thy will ! give us the means of
sweeping sin from off the face of the earth,
so shall thy immortal souls not be lost to
thee for ever, so shall no power be greater
than thine own.' But we have our answer :
' My thoughts are not your thoughts, neither
are your ways my ways,' saith the
Lord.

When Enid Osborn heard that Ellis's wife
was under the same roof with herself, she
resolved upon seeing her, and telling her

personally what she had made known to her husband just six weeks ago. Ellis had not heeded it much ; he had refused to interfere, saying that Zaré knew her own business best, but Enid was sure she did not know that these so-called friends were deceiving her, cheating her, ruining her ; Enid could prove it, and she felt bound to do so. It would lose her her comfortable place, it would leave the little Princess Loyella friendless again ; but Ellis's wife must be saved, Ellis must be saved through her. Enid felt sure that if once Zaré's faith in this false friend were overthrown, she would go back to Ellis, and by her lifelong devotion atone to him for the little love she had shown him of late ; that her old affection for him, which Enid saw had been destroyed by the unwholesome influence this princess exercised over her, would return when that influence should cease.

So Enid, having once resolved, let no time pass before putting her plan into execution.

On the very first evening of Zaré's coming to the princess's house ; late, when Zaré had retired to her own room tired with her day's journey ; when the prince and princess were out at a public dinner, forgetting in the blaze of light and colour, under the influence of wine and music, their *cara amica* at home, Enid went downstairs and knocked gently at Zaré's bedroom door.

' Come in,' said a weary voice, thinking it was one of the servants ; and Enid went in and stood before Ellis's wife once more, as she had done in the parlour of the cottage at Littlefield two years ago.

They had both changed: Zaré was a thousandfold less beautiful than she had been then, Enid a thousandfold more so; more Madonna-like, more heart-stirring, because of the melancholy which played cadence-like on her eyes and lips.

Mrs. Lyndon did not recognise her in the dim light; she had no suspicion that the governess of whom the princess had often spoken in such high terms of praise was in very truth the woman who stood, as Zaré believed, between herself and her husband's love.

Enid had been with her when she was ill in Baden-Baden, but Zaré remembered nothing of that time; she had not known her then, or any person, or anything which had surrounded her. It was because Enid felt sure of this that she had come to enlighten her now, come to save Ellis's wife, who had had so little pity for her. Enid did not know that Zaré had seen her on her last visit to Ellis at his studio—a visit made as purely for Zaré's sake as was this to her room now.

Zaré was sitting by the fire. It was the end of June, but cold—one of those cheerless days we often get in summer. Zaré was cold, like the day, for she bent over the grate holding her long white hands out to the blaze.

She did not look up when Enid went over and stood by her side, feeling sure that it was only one of the servants come to ask about her general habits : what time she would rise, or where breakfast, or whether she required help.

' Can you afford me ten minutes' undivided attention, Mrs. Lyndon ?' Enid asked.

Zaré looked up now, and recognised the woman she had left standing side by side with Ellis before the picture in the studio. She fancied she was delirious, that the spectre of that horrible day, and others following it, was haunting her still. She sprang up from her chair and caught hold of the mantelshelf.

' Who are you ? why do you follow me here ?' she gasped, as if she were addressing one of the ghosts which had pursued her of late.

' I am Enid Osborn ; you must remember me ; you cannot have forgotten coming to visit me at Littlefield. At the present moment I am a governess in this house.' Then, after a pause, ' Mrs. Lyndon, I have lately learnt something which materially affects yourself; I would tell you, and warn you, if you will hear me. I believe it to be a matter of great importance to your future happiness.'

'Sit down,' said Zaré, recovering, and resuming her old queenly dignity of manner. She was not afraid of her enemy, now she knew it to be a mortal one. It could not hurt her to listen to what Enid would say; probably it was some miserable excuse for, or explanation of, her conduct of last month, at which Zaré's lip would only curl in silent scorn. She had always been generous to an adversary, particularly a weak one, and Zaré knew that she had taken a glorious revenge, that she had slain them both—him first, and this woman he loved by his side. He would not care for anything in this world again;

love would be a meaningless term for him in future.

But she would listen to Enid's story. So she motioned her to a chair, and sat down opposite to her. Enid suspected nothing; she had always seen Ellis's wife in this haughty. condescending mood, treating her as though she were only some helpless bird trembling in her grasp.

But Enid had set herself a task ; it was for Ellis's sake, not Zaré's, she worked. She saw how wretched these two were, how far apart, and she knew that the Princess of La Viola stood between them. But she had learnt something which must surely remove this stumbling-block to their peace. Zaré could no longer love or trust the princess, or be led by her, when she should have heard all Enid could tell. She would surely go back

to Ellis, and take back with her the old love
of which the princess had tried to rob him
for the accomplishment of her own avaricious
desires.

'You may speak,' Zaré said, seeing that
Enid was silent; 'I can give you my utmost
attention.   There is nothing to distract my
thoughts.   I shall *understand* what you say
perfectly.'

She laid a great stress on the word 'understand,' intending Enid to see that it would
be impossible to mislead her, or blind her. Enid
must have been dreaming, for it conveyed no
meaning to her mind.   She was only thinking how to begin her story, it being a difficult subject to handle, and painful withall.

'Have you any remembrance of the time
when you were so ill in the Princess of La
Viola's house in Baden-Baden?' Enid began

presently, thinking a question would open the way for her.

'None ; nor do I wish to be told of anything which went on at that time. I was a fool, and I paid the penalty of my credulity. Like many others, I acted up to my faith, I trusted in my own belief. It proved a false one. I sacrificed to it all I cared for in the world, and I found myself deceived. I confess my own weakness, but I will not be taunted with it by you or any one. If you came to *argue for him* on the old subject of my *palazzo*, I must recall my permission and request you to leave me.'

Enid heard the stress on the words 'argue for him,' but still they conveyed no distinct meaning. She was too much absorbed in her own subject.

'You mistake me,' she said gently ; 'I did

not mean to speak about your *palazzo.*
Perhaps if I come to the point at once, it
will prevent misunderstandings. When you
were ill in Baden-Baden, have you any remembrance of making a will, or signing one,
or something of the kind, in your bedroom in
the princess's house, with the old servants,
Pietro and Ella, as witnesses, and some
German lawyer or attorney — I know
nothing about these people, but I mean
some foreigner to manage all the business
for you ?'

' What are you talking about, child ? You
are mad ; I never made a will of any kind—
never in my life ; explain yourself.'

' I suspected that you were not conscious
of what went on around you, because you did
not even know me, and I was constantly by
your side.'

'You ! and you saw me make a will ?' Zaré asked, in a voice of exceeding terror, half starting out of her seat.

'No—not I.' A pause. Zaré seemed relieved, and sat down again. 'I did not suspect anything wrong at the time, knowing nothing of the people amongst whom I had come. Had I known then, I should have warned your husband when he came to fetch you, but——'

'You will oblige me by not bringing his name into the subject; he has nothing to do with my affairs, as you know,' Zaré interrupted proudly. Then, with a satirical smile, 'And who has found intellectual amusement for himself or herself in inventing this talented romance about *a will?*'

'Old Ella told me she was herself a witness to your signature of one, as you lay in your bed fever-stricken. Later the princess turned Ella out of the house in a passion, and then the poor woman came to me. She begged me, if I ever saw you again, to ask whether you had intended to sign this will, or any will. She suspected something wrong, and she asked me to warn you by telling you what she had seen. Since she left, I have understood broken snatches of conversation between the prince and princess, which would have been perfectly meaning-less to me had I not heard old Ella's story.'

'And what do you suspect? For God's sake tell me!'

Zaré was pale as death now; her teeth were chattering like one in an ague fit.

'I have no right to tell you mere sus-picions. I have stated a fact, that Ella saw you sign a will of some kind in your bedroom at Baden-Baden. That she spoke the truth I judge from my own hearing later. I know nothing more. I should not even have suspected any wrong in the fact of your signing a will when you were ill, had I not felt sure that you were at the time only in a semi-conscious condition, and certainly not responsible for, or cognizant of, your own actions. Had it been otherwise, you would have known who I was.'

'And you nursed me—you, Enid Osborn ?'

'Yes, but that is not a part of the question. You are in perfect possession of your senses now, and if you think these people have wronged you, you will take some trouble to find out. It may not be an easy matter—every word they speak to you is a lie ; I hear the true state of their feelings behind your back. They have no suspicion that I am in any way acquainted with you or yours ; they discuss you unreservedly before me, for I and the little Princess Loyella dine at their luncheon table. I do not wish to abuse them ; they have always treated me well, but I have thought a great deal about this matter, and I am sure they are false to you — both of them.'

There was a long silence. Zaré sat with her hands clasped in one another, and her teeth firm - set together. At last she said :

'I feel bound to thank you for your warning ; the intention may be kind, but I cannot tell you that I absolutely believe my oldest friend a liar and a thief, and she must be both if what you say prove to be the truth. She could have only one object in making me sign a will—the will only one meaning. But I will not judge her hastily. Old Ella may be in her dotage, or she may have a grudge against Nicoline.'

' I do not wish you to accept any one's assertion ; I only wish to warn you, that you may find out for yourself. I don't know whether your husband told you that I had called at your house about six or seven weeks ago to beg him to explain all this ; it would have come better from him than from me, but he said you disliked interference in your private affairs. Accordingly I determined on telling you myself. I knew you would return to the princess as soon as you were quite recovered ; I heard her say you had promised to do so.

I have waited, oh so anxiously! for your coming.'

Zaré allowed her to finish speaking, and then she came over and stood before her, bending her neck slightly, so that the fire of her eyes might fall straight down upon Enid, and scorch her with their passionate flame.

'Perhaps you are not aware, Miss Osborn, that I *saw* you at my house? It is quite superfluous to explain what brought you there. This is the second time I have come upon you unawares and seen my husband bending over you, touching you, and talking to you in low loving tones. Your excuse for this affectionate sympathy, mutual love for *his picture*,' with a sneer. 'I heard him tell you that—the eyes were yours—the expression yours—and perhaps you think that I, his wife, would stand calmly by and see him become famous for your sake. Once he told me that you had saved him from despair;' with a cruel laugh, 'go and do so now, if you can. I will grant you the victory. I will crown you with my own hand, if you can do more for him than I have done.' A pause. '*I have destroyed that picture,*' she said at last, with a devilish intensity ; ' Get him to paint another—If you can.'

Zaré ceased speaking ; she did not move away, but stood there side by side with the trembling Enid, her jewels flashing in the firelight, and her white teeth gleaming.

Enid did not know what to answer or how to act. Ellis's words that Zaré was jealous of her came back upon her memory, and she saw that they had not been said in jest.

Her first impulse was to rise and leave the
room, nor stoop to self-justification.   But
again her love for Ellis ruled her, making
her sink her own identity, compelling her to
forget herself.   It was she who stood between
Ellis and his wife, after all.   This magnificent
woman by her side fancied the artist, the adorer
of beauty, cared more for a pale sad face than
for all that glow and colour, cared more for
a little unaccomplished country girl than for
the talent and brilliancy of this splendid
woman whom he had married !   It seemed
a marvel to Enid that Zaré could doubt her
own power over him ; but it was so, evidently.
For Ellis's sake she must remove this doubt,
she must inflict upon herself one last, one
greatest pang.   For his sake she must subdue
her natural anger at the accusation, she must
argue with Zaré and persuade her, she must

use her whole intellect to assume an influence over the mind of the angry woman at her side, the woman who was—*jealous of her*.

Enid could almost have smiled at the wildness of the imagining. But Ellis was suffering. Zaré must be brought back to him; she must undo what she had done, she must lead him upwards again, as she had led him before, but with greater love and tenderer pity, in atonement of the wrong she had inflicted. Enid said it should be so, and she was not infirm of purpose, or of feeble intellect; she saw through the whole affair from the beginning until now, and she understood whence the mistake had arisen. It was not so unnatural, after all.

Enid therefore made no outward sign of the anger she felt at Zaré's accusation. Her face had flushed to a vivid scarlet, but it paled again, and she was calm; she also rose from her seat, and standing by Zaré's side, laid her little hand upon that of her enemy as it rested on the chimney-piece.

'Mrs. Lyndon,' she said, very slowly, and in a deep intense voice, 'you are generous, and you are true. You do not lie yourself—you would scorn to stoop to such meanness. You do not believe that every one else is a liar. You would at least give me credit for telling you the truth, whatever that truth might be. Tell me—Will you believe me if I speak on my word of honour? or if not, I will take a solemn oath before heaven and before you, Ellis's wife, that I speak the simple and un-swerving truth, that I will not deceive you in any one point. Say, will you believe me ?'

'You need take no oath, child ; truth is written in your eyes, on your lips. I saw it there when first I met you, and it being so, I know what you will tell me. Remember, I accuse you of no *sin*, but only of having wronged me by allowing your old love for each other to find expression now. Had *you* not come across his path, he would have been true to me ; for he did love me—yes, I tell you, he loved me ; I did not lie to you—he loved me when I married him.'

There was a wail of agony in the last words which brought the tears into Enid's eyes.

'I will not argue with you yet,' she said. 'I will first make a statement, speaking to you as from woman to woman, as from one

who would scorn a lie, to another who would
scorn a lie. If you believe me—we are both
saved; if you will not—you must be un-
generous enough to suppose me guilty of
what you would not be guilty yourself;
you must give me the lie to my face, and—
I must leave you. Listen to me, Mrs.
Lyndon, I speak in all good faith. When
you came to me and told me that Ellis
Lyndon had never loved me, that I had
mistaken him, I knew you spoke the truth;
I could recall all his words and actions, and
I saw that they were not as mine were, that
there was no love in them. There was not
then, and there never has been. I stood to
him only in the place of a sister, and as such
I still stand. We have known each other
from childhood; as boy and girl we have
kissed each other, and struck each other, and

kissed again—hated one another, and loved one another, according to the mood of the moment.

'Can you wonder, then, that when he meets me now, forgetting that mistake of mine and his, which for a time made us something different, he should only too gladly have gone back to his old boyish intimacy with me, that he should sit near me, or take my hand, or lay his arm upon my shoulder, as you saw him doing? But it was not love—no, Mrs. Lyndon; he has never spoken a loving word to me, never one that you might not have sat by and heard—never since I first bade him set me free from my promise to be his wife. Give me your hands—both of them—look into my eyes and tell me—Am I lying to you?'

Her deep truthful eyes were raised straight to Zaré's face, her sweet lips parted in prayer-like supplication. There was something so firm and true in the pressure with which she grasped Zaré's unwilling hands, that the strong woman trembled before her. She could not say 'You lie!' yet she dared not believe Enid spoke the truth, for if it were the truth, what did it leave her—Zaré? The thought was madness; she could only say :

'But you—you loved him.'

'I did, *I do*,' Enid answered, brave as a young Indian chief at the stake. 'I will not lie to you, not in one single instance. I will not deceive you, even to protect myself from your scorn. Since I *did* love him *then*, I *do* love him *now;* we change our natures— we cannot undo what is done, but we *can* hide it. We cannot blind ourselves, but we can blind others. I was taught the meaning of the word honour, Mrs. Lyndon; my father taught it me. I hold my own too sacred a thing to blemish it for a momentary gratification. I know what is due to myself, I know what is due to you. In dishonouring you I must dishonour myself tenfold. I have neither been guilty of one nor the other. From the moment I learnt that Ellis had never loved me, from the moment I *knew* it was so by my own feelings, I swore to myself that my love, which seemed now a shame to me, should be for ever hidden from him. He should think me like himself, he should fancy that he, too, had made a mistake, and that my supposed love for him had only been a girl's passing fancy. I have succeeded; he often taxes me with a want even of that old sisterly friendship which has always existed between us. I may have over-acted my part, I may have given him unnecessary pain by too great coldness, but I have *not* forgotten my own honour, never for one single moment. Had he not been married, my pride would still have made me conceal my miserable, one-sided love. He would never have known it, even had you not stood between us, provided I had ever learnt my silly, childish mistake as to his feelings. But enough, I have never betrayed myself by word or look, and he has nothing to betray. Do I speak the truth ? I can say no more, I can prove nothing; but as you would judge yourself, so I leave you to judge me and him. He is no liar either; ask him whether he loves me—there will be no hesitation in his answer. Why have you not gone to him and taxed him with loving me ? It would have been the more generous proceeding on your part.'

Again her eyes were raised to Zaré's, clear and truthful and lovely ; but Zaré's proud head was sinking lower and lower. She caught hold of the chimney-piece to keep herself from falling. She must be strong for one more moment, she must get the girl out of her room—no one must be witness to her humiliation. So she grasped the shelf, and half leaning against it, said, in broken gasps :

' I am not feeling quite well, Miss Osborn ; leave me for a while, please ; we will talk of this again, at another time—Forgive my hasty accusation—I will consider what you have said—Thank you for your warning about the will—*I never made one;* good-night.'

She held out her hand, trying not to show how it was trembling. There was the same haughty grace about her, the same glorious pride of bearing, even in her fall.

Enid never forgot her as she had left her standing there, self-condemned—with an agony unspeakable written on evey feature, as the red light of the fire blazed and flickered and played upon her face, like a reflection of the hell which was burning within her. With her diamonds flashing and sparkling in the fitful light, and her white bosom heaving; with the long classic drapery of her purple velvet dress falling about her, and the ruddy coils of her hair, like a gold crown around her head. Yes, it was a picture of sun-illumined ruin and jewel-covered desolation which Enid never forgot.

As soon as her visitor left the room, Zaré rushed to the door, turned the key in the lock, and fell upon her knees by the bedside, hiding her face in the coverings. Her frame was shaken by sobs, which seemed to tear her in pieces with their violence.

'What have I done?' she uttered aloud at intervals. 'Oh God! Oh God!' and then she lay grovelling on the ground. 'There is truth in her eyes! truth in her voice! Why did I not go to her before; she would have stayed my hand. It is too late now—too late!' Zaré almost screamed, beating her hands upon the carpet, and writhing like an injured serpent in her misery. Then she lay still for several moments, stiff and cold, like one dead.

But suddenly she arose, and with an almost

superhuman effort checked the outward expression of her emotion. She had decided
upon some course of action, she must to work
at once.

If she let herself break down, they would
conquer her, these false friends; they, at
least, should have no triumph in her fall.
She must be strong for yet a little while, she
must be up and doing, even now, before the
night should come upon her, in which no
man can work.

First she opened her desk and wrote two
letters; one was very long, and one short.
These she stamped and laid on her table
whilst she changed her dress. She moved
quickly, as though it were a matter of life
or death to her, this race with time. She put
on the darkest and least conspicuous clothes
she could find, and when bonneted and

cloaked, Zaré crept softly down the stairs, and passed out at the front door.

It was only eight o'clock—She would probably find the man she wanted at his office still. He would do anything to oblige her, she knew he would work all night if need be ; he was on old and faithful friend. She hailed a hansom, and drove to his chambers in Lincoln's Inn.

Her only terror was lest she should die before she reached her lawyer. She had a sort of desperate notion that the winged Nemesis was chasing her, sword in hand, to wreak a mighty vengeance upon her, and that her hours were numbered. She did not care—she only strained every nerve and sinew to reach Lincoln's Inn ; she only prayed to find the old lawyer at home. After that, let what might fall upon her, they should never say she had been duped, cheated, taken in like a poor silly child.

She—who had made a boast of her own far-seeing intellect !

CHAPTER VIII.

IT was the day after Ellis Lyndon had been talking of his future to Fred Galway with the reckless despairing of a ruined life, that the following letter reached him; and even before he had finished reading it a telegram from the princess followed with the words :

'Come to my house at once ; Zaré is dead.'

The letter had prepared him for the news.

It had been written and posted by her own hand, while yet the deed now done was only contemplated.

'Ellis, my husband, forgive me. I die with this prayer upon my lips. Before my letter reaches you I shall be lying cold and hideous to look upon. *I*—there is no such thing ; what I sprang from, to that I have returned, and that is impersonal and unconscious.

'It was to get rid of my identity that I have sacrificed my life. I hated myself, I despised myself, I could not endure such an existence. I have put an end to it—And it were well for me if this were all I have done ; you will pardon my weakness, but you will never pardon my crime. Oh God ! if I had slain myself alone, there would be mercy for me yet, mercy in oblivion, rest in death ; but you live, you cannot forget ; I have murdered your body, and cast your soul into hell. I have desecrated your altar, I have been untrue to my own faith, and false to the gods I had worshipped. I, who sacrificed at the shrine of art, bowing my knee, and pledging to it the devotion of my life ; I have forsworn myself, I am a traitor and a coward. There is no power on earth which will undo what I have done, nothing which can reinstate me in my own self-respect. But I can refuse to sit by and witness my own degradation—*I have refused;* I have chosen death rather.

'But you, Ellis, you live—Will you ever believe that through it all I loved you? Surely my jealousy proves it ; we cannot be jealous where there is no love, for jealousy

hath its mainspring in love. I make no excuse ; there is none to make. I was mad,
wicked, despicable ; I know myself now, as
you must have known me then.

' You will wonder what power on all this
earth was mighty enough in its working to
make me—Zaré—acknowledge that I was
wrong ; self-deluded, self-slain by my own
passions, which, from my birth, were laid as
a curse upon me. It was a simple enough
cause, too, which produced this wondrous
effect—only a pair of truthful, childlike eyes
raised fearlessly to mine, Ellis ; only pure
young lips speaking to me like the voice of
one of Raphael's angels, uttering simple
words of which it were a crime to doubt
the truth. Only two little hands clasping
mine in tenderness and absolute faith. Only
Enid Osborn herself—a child whose bare, un-

proven statement I have accepted as my own death-warrant.

'But make no mistake, Ellis, my end lies not on her head. I would have lived and returned to you, and begged mercy, grovelling at your feet, had not my hands been dyed with the life-blood of your soul. Had I not destroyed your picture—I know what that means; I knew it then. There is no atonement for such a crime—no forgiveness to ask or hope for. I know what I have made of you, of the only man I ever loved; I can see your future life, all in horrible distinctness, drawn out before my mind's eye. I see a vast genius lost—for ever lost—to all mankind. I see one more great mind dying in its infancy. And I have done this—oh God! oh God!

'But enough!—regrets are unavailing. I

would still ask a favour at your hands, even as the condemned criminal before the judgment seat; it is that you will accept from me the few treasures I have still remaining. My house in London and all it contains, and everything that has been mine. The money is not enough to embarrass you. I have squandered the greater part of my once vast fortune. There is scarcely over two thousand pounds a year coming from my present capital, but it is yours, Ellis. I know you will accept it; you cannot refuse me the gratification of my last wish.

'If the Princess of La Viola produces a will of mine (which I have reason to believe she will), it is useless, it is a forgery; but you can prove that there is a later one—I made it only yesterday. It is in the hands of our old friend, Paul Haughton; he was one of the few people you respected and trusted ; he will explain all to you.

'Promise me, Ellis, that you will not allow the Princess of La Viola, whom I have at last seen in her true colours, to glory over my death, and to take possession of my property. It is a sacred trust which I give into *your* hands ; you cannot, you will not, refuse to except it when the law puts it into your keeping.

'If by any chance the princess does not bring forward a will of mine, there is only one extant—that which I made last night. If she does, the existence of this later one annuls all her claims. Remember, Ellis, I never made the one she will produce, although I believe it was signed by my own hand. The whole business was a fraud. You must not let her triumph in successful crime. You must produce my last will. Two other people know of the princess's attempt to rob me; I have written to them also, so the affair will not lie solely in your hands.

'You see, I have made every arrangement for my death. I do not shrink from what I am about to do. To-night as the clock strikes twelve, I shall swallow the dose which will lay me into my last long sleep, from which there will be no awaking to a knowledge of degradation and misery. The conscious *I* will be an unconscious nullity. If perchance my spirit progresses towards eternity in the general progression of all created things, I have but set it free to begin that outward movement a day or two, or a year or two, before nature would have done it for me.

'I do not believe in eternal punishment,

as you know, Ellis, our punishment and our rewards are all contained in the sum of this world's good—not individual good, but collective; not your happiness or mine, but the welfare, and through that, the happiness of all mankind. I grant my death a crime—it is a coward's act; but after all I am only a woman.

' May you, for the honour of your manhood, have greater courage, Ellis; or if such a thing be possible to you, have greater faith, so shall you not perish as I have done. If—oh, Heavens!—*if* you have the strength to rise again from the blow which my hand has dealt you, then were your reward a mighty one indeed; then were the strength of your own will a pride and a glory in all the coming years—a thing to hold up before the face of a future generation, saying :

' "See! there is no power on earth which will lay genius under the sod. Its progressive and expansive force is infinite: the earth will not withhold it, nor the waters, nor the fires; it is unconsumable, imperishable! The germs of its life are indestructible; you may wither them for a time, and make them unfruitful, but see! they rise again and defy you."

' Ellis! think of the glorious triumph which will be yours if you can prove that the genius in you was no poor mortal body to perish at a blow, but a mighty and immortal power, issuing from, and partaking of the nature of, that Almighty force which governs the universe. Think of it, Ellis! bind up your strength, put your foot upon the devil's neck and set his power at naught. See, I am already grovelling at your feet—spurn me, defy me, and let all honest men see your victory.

'Ellis, these are the last words I shall ever speak to you. Do not let a woman's hand have had the power to slay you. Assert your manhood, display your strength, and conquer yet; so shall my poor tortured spirit rest quietly in its unhallowed grave.

'ZARÉ.'

Even as Ellis finished reading this letter there were loud knockings at the door—noisy rushings to and fro, servants talking excitedly in the passages, and hurried messages brought to him.

The princess had sent her carriage; would he come at once?—they could do nothing without him.

41—2

Do!—what was there to do? The end
had come at last, his own and hers; Fate
was determined to sweep all traces of his
life off the face of the earth.

But he went to the princess's house, feeling
a strange desire to be certain that Zaré was
actually dead. He could not believe it. She
had seemed the sort of being who could never
die, the essence of a strong enduring nature
which nothing could quell. He could not
picture her bright passion-glowing eyes dull
and expressionless, her warm lips cold and
colourless; he could not imagine her dead—
he must see to believe.

So, in the glare of the midday sunlight,
he stood beside her once again, alone. They
had dressed her lifeless body in its richest
clothes, and decked it with its costliest jewels.
It was a custom of their family with the

dead, to dress it out, and let it lie in all its glory till the coffin should take it from their sight; they had treated Zaré as one of themselves.

It is as well to honour your victim; and they fancied themselves so safe, now she was dead—Poor fools!—they were soon enough undeceived. Let us say no more about them—their crime never came before the public. Ellis showed them more mercy than they had shown to him or her.

Presently as he looked at her lying there so helpless, a sort of pity stole for an instant into his hardened heart. He bent towards her, and wished to seal the bond of his forgiveness by laying a kiss upon her still beautiful brow. But ere his lips touched her, he drew back— a shudder passed through his frame, and he turned away.

No! it was not possible to feel tender, even towards the poor harmless corpse; it was still Zaré, the incarnate fiend in woman's guise who had taken from him, with relentless hand, everything for which he had lived and struggled and hoped; who had torn him down from the height on which he stood, left him lifeless on the ground, and gloried at the work she had done.

Ellis could not kiss her—it were an acted lie to make believe that he could forgive or forget, even for a moment. No; the iron had entered into his soul and driven out of it all human softness, all manly pity. He turned away without even touching the beautiful hand which lay covered with jewels on the coverlet—turned away with loathing from the creature for whom only so short a time ago his whole being had burned with intense love; from lips on which his own had pressed the first passionate kisses of a young man's perfected nature—kisses which are never given again to any woman, let him love as often as he may.

It is never *the first* again—never the first glorious consciousness of his own manhood, the feeling that he loves and is beloved, as it dawns in all its vividness on the hitherto sombre sky of a young man's existence. Ellis Lyndon had felt it in all its intensity—the contrast of his past and his present was doubly revolting.

He left the room and he left the house, stealing out like a thief, creeping softly down the stairs lest they should hear him—those who were waiting for him in the drawing-room. He could not face them; they were a part of the evil of his life. Their hands had wrought the first crooked meshes of the net which had tangled itself round his feet, and stopped his further progress for ever and for ever. They had made it, and Zaré had thrown it, and together they had succeeded splendidly in breaking the wings of the poor bird which had flown so blindly into it, attracted by the delicious bait they laid for him.

He could almost believe now that the whole thing was but some devil's wiles, such as Mephistopheles had used to lure Faust to his destruction ; to bring down to the level of the grossest things of earth the high-soaring intellect—down to the confines of hell itself.

And so he passed out from amongst them. He had seen no one : they had allowed him to go unmolested to the audience chamber of death ; hoping to speak with him afterwards ; but they waited in vain—he never came. He only went to visit his old friend Paul Haughton, to hear what he could tell, and to leave all business matters in his hands. He wrote but two letters, one to Fred Galway, begging him to accept a few hundred pounds from him as a fond remembrance of all the kindness he had shown to his thankless cousin ; and one letter to Enid, telling her that he was going away—going to lose his own identity in the wilds of America or Australia, going to become a wanderer on the face of the earth for the rest of his days.

She could do nothing for him now, he said ; even her sympathy, once so precious, could not save him from himself. He despised himself for the weakness of his own nature ; but since such was his nature, how could he change it ? Enid must forget him ; let him pass out of her life as though no such creature had ever entered into it.

Then early one morning he sailed away ; out of the life-teeming London Docks, out of the smoke of the city, out on to the broad ocean where no one knew him ; where the sky and the waters, the beasts, the birds, the fishes, would henceforth be the only friends who should claim his sympathies.

And that was the end.

It is only a life which I have written—a wrecked and ruined life—A mighty intellect and great desires crushed from the moment of their birth—a strange sympathetic nature driven with stripes and lashes away from all human fellowship, even in the days of its infancy.

We, who have the sympathy of our brothers and our sisters, of our mothers, our wives, our children; we do not know what isolation means—how utter is the desolation of the heart which lacks a fellow-creature's love, how empty the life which is filled only with itself. We do not know how unattainable those desires which have no bond of human sympathy held out to lead them upwards; how, left alone, they turn to gall and bitterness, and wither up the spirit which gave them birth.

It was for lack of sympathy that Ellis Lyndon fell; because no man or woman had ever known him; because all his affections had been driven back upon himself one after the other as they sprang into life; even from that day when, with child-like faith and a child's yearning for sympathy, he had carried his little picture of God and the Angels to his mother in triumphant expectation of her praise, and lo !—she had thrown it into the fire before his eyes because the subject was ' impious '—so she said, not understanding the boy had believed it a sacred work, like the glass windows in the church, which he loved to stare at all service time.

That was the beginning—And this the end.

The genius within him had lived again and flourished for a season as the sunlight of love shone upon it. Then, when one sudden withering lightning flash seared up everything which lay around and about him, striking him to the ground—afterwards, I say, when he rose again, and saw the desolation, and found himself standing alone in its midst, he had neither the desire nor the power to seek out another resting-place. So he stood there and let the tempest rage around him. The winds blew him whither they would, and the waters covered him; he only shivered helplessly—as he had shivered when they tore his pet dog, the one creature who loved him, out of his little clinging arms and had it killed—'To teach him a wholesome moral lesson.' It had failed in its object, and succeeded in another — in hardening the child's heart, in turning his young affections into a source of misery to himself, so that he said :

' I will learn to care for nothing in this world — no animate creature. Inanimate things cannot misunderstand me; of them alone will I make my friends.'

And so the child clung fondly to his books. But nature had given him warm human passions, which occasionally burnt furiously

within him, or broke out into open flame.
The most violent of these natural convulsions
was his love for Zaré Landrelle. But even
that was turned to gall and bitterness by the
knowledge of her vices. He had brought
the curse upon himself; it was a just punishment for his mad folly in marrying such a
woman. But he could have borne with her,
and with himself then, for another passion, a
nobler, a grander desire, was ruling his life.
Art had become his wife, his child, his strong
castle of defence; for it alone he lived, in its
existence he existed, it had become a part of
his very being. When it was severed from
him it was as the severance of the soul from
the body, there was no reuniting them.

There are men who have strength enough
to withstand such a blow, men who could
calmly take up brush and box and begin all

over again; smiling at a woman's futile attempt to conquer genius, scoffing at the notion that a man's intellect can be slain at one thrust, however cleverly dealt, however sharp the weapon. 'It is immortal,' they say, 'and indestructible.'

Ellis Lyndon was not of these. He had one stronghold to which he clung in absolute faith and perfect trust; it was wrenched from him; he could not build up for himself another, he had no desire even to try. It was a weakness of his nature; he was no hero —And so the end came.—The world never knew him. His was only one more human mind which has existed and perished, and no one has known that it ever aspired to anything beyond the safe keeping of the body in which it was enshrined.

And so men live and die, and 'All things

are flowing onward, and every shape is assumed in a fleeting course. Even Time itself glides on with a constant progress, no otherwise than a river. For neither can the river nor the fleeting hour stop in its course, but as wave is impelled by wave, and the one before is pressed on by that which follows, and itself presses on that before it, so do the moments fly on, so do they follow, and so are they ever renewed. For the moment which was before is passed, and that which was not, *now* exists, and every minute is re-placed.'*

＊　　　＊　　　＊　　　＊　　　＊

Long years afterwards, ten or twelve perhaps—Ellis Lyndon had kept no account of the passage of time—by one of those strange turns of destiny which we all

* Pythagoras.

experience, he came face to face with Enid Osborn again; met her far from their native land in an Australian settlement, whither she had gone as governess to an English family when she left the Princess of La Viola after Zaré's death. They were both past their youth then; he was weary of his aimless wanderings, sick unto death of his objectless life, tired, and longing for rest.

After infinite trouble he persuaded Enid to become his wife. He could not talk to her of a young passionate love, he could only ask her for mercy, implore her to come forward and save him now, before he should abandon himself to utter despair, pray her to give him something for which to keep his self-respect, his manhood, ere it should go from him with all the rest.

Enid was a true woman, with a woman's

loving weakness. Her old passionate fondness for him had died out during the passage of the years; but she had never loved another, and her tenderness for him was perfect. How could she see him perish for lack of that care which she could give him? There was no self-sacrifice needed for the deed; she would have desired no better destiny for the filling up of her own empty life; she could bear with him, and be gentle with his faults, remembering his sufferings, the bitterness of which she had not known till now. She had only wondered why his name had never reached her ears, but supposed she was too far removed from the great world of civilisation for its light to reach her. Yet she heard other artists' names breathed with respect and pride by their fellow countrymen here in the new Australian colony, but never his; never that for which she listened, and looked, and pined, till every tender sentiment wore itself out with unsatisfied longing. Then she ceased to regret; she almost forgot that a past had ever existed for her; she lived on from day to day, peacefully content in the pleasures which the moment brought to her, thankful that her lines had been cast in pleasant places. And so she passed out of her young womanhood quietly and with no regret.

It was then she met him again, then she became his wife, living with him in the new country which became their own and their children's after them. They had money enough to have abode in cities and enjoyed society, but they laid it aside for their children's future use; Zaré's money, which he *could not* touch. They were tillers of

42—2

the soil, labourers in the field of a new kingdom all their own, to govern as they would. And the law of their land was perfect liberty of thought, absolute justice, unfailing sympathy, and unswerving faith. That is what they taught their children, and the result was perfect love, and peace, and unity in the home which Enid Lyndon governed.

THE END.

[*For Public Reading.*]

'HEARTLESS DOT.'

ONE OF ELLIS LYNDON'S SOUL-STIRRING SKETCHES.

HEARTLESS DOT.

It was only a sketch they showed me. Nothing but a rough-headed, wondering-eyed child, with a toy spade in his hand, and a scared look over his face, standing on a mound of newly-turned earth, and digging, digging, for dear life. The golden hues of the sunset glowed behind him, and the blackness of night lay in front; overhead were two bats chasing a big white moth, so fearless of the child's presence that they seemed like to tangle their wings in his fuzzy hair. It was only Dot—'Heartless

Dot'—and nobody feels any interest in him.
But listen to the story.

'Dot was a wicked child,' they said; 'he
always laughed when good boys cried, and
made a noise when right-minded children
were silent—especially in church.

'You'll come to the gallows some day!'
they told him once, driven to evil prophecy
by his naughtiness. Dot rather hoped he
might, being possessed with an impish curi-
osity to know what it would feel like, to be
swung in the air by your neck, 'ever, ever so
high up!'—But all this is wandering, it had
nothing to do with the sketch; only we are
told that the past is the best prophet of the
future. It may be so. Who can tell?

There came a day whereon a shadow lay
over the home in which Dot lived. It was
the angel with the amaranthine wreath who,

' pausing, descended, and, with voice divine,
whispered a word that had a sound like
death.' Dot's elder brother stood hesitating
on the threshold of eternity.

There was silence all over the house. Even
the children huddled together in a corner,
trembling at the ghostly flutter of the angel's
spirit-wings. Only Dot, heartless Dot,
could not be awed, but danced with cruel
mockery, and sang and laughed around his
wooden horse lying dead on the floor.

' Don't you know,' the nurse said to him
in sepulchral tones of mystic horror, calculated to freeze his young blood, strong with
the fulness of life. ' Don't you know your
poor dear brother is dying.'

' Is he?' said Dot, open-mouthed and joyful ;
' I wants to see him die.'

' He has no more heart than a stone,' the

nurse exclaimed, and turned away despairing.

After that the house was darkened, the
blinds were all drawn down, lest well-inten-
tioned nature should perchance peep into the
rooms with her bright face and laugh at
human woe.

But Dot rebelled against being *compelled*
to sadness while the sun was shining so
kindly, and he angrily tore down the blind
from his nursery window.

'But your poor brother is dead,' they told
him.

'And so's my poor horsey,' Dot answered,
'and he wants the sun to make him live
again.'

And then he danced anew, and clapped his
hands, for the bright beams were pouring in
upon him, and kissing his rough head

lovingly, so that when the nurse said
'Hush!' he mocked her with a shout.

And again, when Dot's brother was being
buried, Dot, peeping under the blind,
laughed at the 'men with flags on their
hats,' danced in his new black shoes 'with
bows on 'em,' and thought a funeral was
'as good *a'most* as a circus.'

'What can we do with him?' his people
asked in despair, turning their thoughts at
last to Dot. 'How can we teach him to
feel?'

'Leave him to me,' the grandmother said,
'I will give him a lesson.'

And so one morning she led him out to
the churchyard, and standing hand in hand
with him by the side of his brother's grave,
she spoke to him in words of mature
wisdom.

'Look there, Dot,' she began, in mild, impressive tones.

Dot stared at the swallows fly-catching above his head.

'Not in the sky, child, there's nothing there.'

Dot looked around him at some butterflies flitting about a rose-bush, and was off, hat in hand to chase them.

'Silly. child !' stopping him. 'Here, at your feet.'

Dot sprung upon a toad, hopping away from a clod, and cuddled it lovingly to his chest. It was taken from him with an exclamation of disgust, and flung far away over the hedge.

'Don't—You hurt it,' screamed the child.

'Never mind the horrid toad, Dot, but listen to me.'

So Dot listened—There might be a story coming.

'Do you see this heap of earth, child? touch it—how cold, and damp, and hard it is! you see, it makes you shiver even to lay your hand upon it. Under this clay your poor dead brother is lying; all night and all day, and always until God shall raise him up to stand before his terrible judgment-seat. And you, Dot, you could laugh, and play, and sing, while the dark hole was being dug, and whilst your own brother was being laid to sleep in the cold hard ground.'

The grandmother looked down at Dot; she would fain mark the effect of her sermon. It was satisfactory. Dot was awed into silence at last, and his big blue eyes seemed trying to fathom the depth of the sod at his feet.

'I likes that story,' he said, finding she had paused. 'Go on.'

Then she told him about heaven and the resurrection, but this he did not like so well; he grew restless, and wanted to go home. So she led him away from the churchyard, and left him alone afterwards to think over the lesson she had read for him.

And Dot acted the whole scene with his wooden horse, alone in the garden.

But later, at eight o'clock, when the children's supper-time came round, Dot was missing. Dot was nowhere to be found; Heartless Dot, who gave them so much trouble, just as they were resting after the fatigues of the miserable week! just as they were forgetting the first agony of their grief for the dead! who, out of sight, was even now passing out of mind. Cruel, Heartless

Dot, who had no more feeling than a stone!

But they were bound to seek him, and after much weary wandering in the fields, and the woods, and the gardens, they found him at last.

He was away in the darkening churchyard, standing on his brother's grave, and with a tiny toy spade, digging, digging, for dear life. The little frightened face glowed red as the sunset sky; the big anxious eyes were fixed upon the clods of earth as they rolled away, one by one, under the push of the bending spade.

'Dot, Dot,' a harsh voice called. 'It's eight o'clock; your supper is all eaten, and you are a wicked boy to frighten us so. What are you doing there?' and a ruthless hand gripped the little arm, dragging the child pitilessly from its standing-place.

Then there arose a shriek which might have rent in twain the heavens and the earth; a cry of anguish, and a passionate protest.

'I *won't* go home! no, no, I won't. I *will* dig him out, I tell you; he is lying there, all down in the cold wet ground; grandmamma said so. The cruel black men put him there, but I'll soon get him out. I'll carry him to my own warm bed and cuddle him up tight. Let me go; let me go.'

And then arose another shriek, followed by a wail of anguish, as they forced him further and further from the spot.

'God will take your brother out,' they told him for consolation.

'But will He now? will He to-night? will He not let him sleep out here in the cold, but bring him back to His warm bed? Will He

not set him up in a great high judgment-
chair, when he's so cold ? will God take care
of him ? will He—will He ?'

But to Dot's pleading there came no other
answer than,

'Come along home do, you bad boy ; how
dare you talk such wicked rubbish ?'

And then again that wail rang out over
the silence of the night, and was echoed only
by the hills.

'Let me go, I *will* dig poor dear brother
out ; nasty, horrid black men to put him
there without any bed to go to sleep in. I
will—I will !'

But alas ! the cry of childhood is impotent ;
the anguish of childhood unheeded. They
do not really feel, we say ! They soon forget !
And people called him 'Heartless Dot' still.

Only the artist read the wordless poem ;

and wrapping the thought about with a purity all its own, caught it while the others stood by unheeding; and giving to it form and substance, heart and soul, made even Dot sublime, even Dot immortal.

THE END.

BILLING AND SONS, PRINTERS, GUILDFORD, SURREY.

www.ingramcontent.com/pod-product-compliance
Lightning Source LLC
Chambersburg PA
CBHW020611030726
47497CB00007B/2185